Praise for Ellie Crowe's books:

"Inspiring and poignant"
—Bloomsbury Press

"Well researched and fact-filled"
—School Library Journal

"Hard to put down"
—Asian American Press

"Page-turning drama"
—The Star Advertiser

"An intense, emotional story"
—The Sacramento Bee

"A gripping and engaging story"
—Online Book Club

*"There were parts of this book that even scared ME,
but it all ends happily."*
—Misty, Hawai'i Book Blog

GatorLands

INDIGORIVER
PUBLISHING

GATORLANDS

ELLIE CROWE

Indigo River Publishing

Worst Summer Ever: Gatorlands
Copyright © 2018 by Ellie Crowe

This book is a work of fiction. Names, characters, locations, and incidents are the product of the author's imagination or are used fictitiously. Any resemblance to actual events or persons, living or dead, is coincidental.

All rights reserved. No portion of this publication may be reproduced, stored in a retrieval system, or transmitted by any means—electronic, mechanical, photocopying, recording, or any other—except for brief quotations in printed reviews, without the prior written permission of the publisher.

Indigo River Publishing
3 West Garden Street, Ste. 352
Pensacola, FL 32502
www.indigoriverpublishing.com

Book Design: Robin Vuchnich
Editors: Rachel Rehr and Regina Cornell

Ordering Information:
Quantity sales: Special discounts are available on quantity purchases by corporations, associations, and others. For details, contact the publisher at the address above.

Orders by U.S. trade bookstores and wholesalers: Please contact the publisher at the address above.

Printed in the United States of America

Library of Congress Control Number: 2018963398

ISBN: 978-1-948080-66-8

First Edition

With Indigo River Publishing, you can always expect great books, strong voices, and meaningful messages. Most importantly, you'll always find . . . words worth reading.

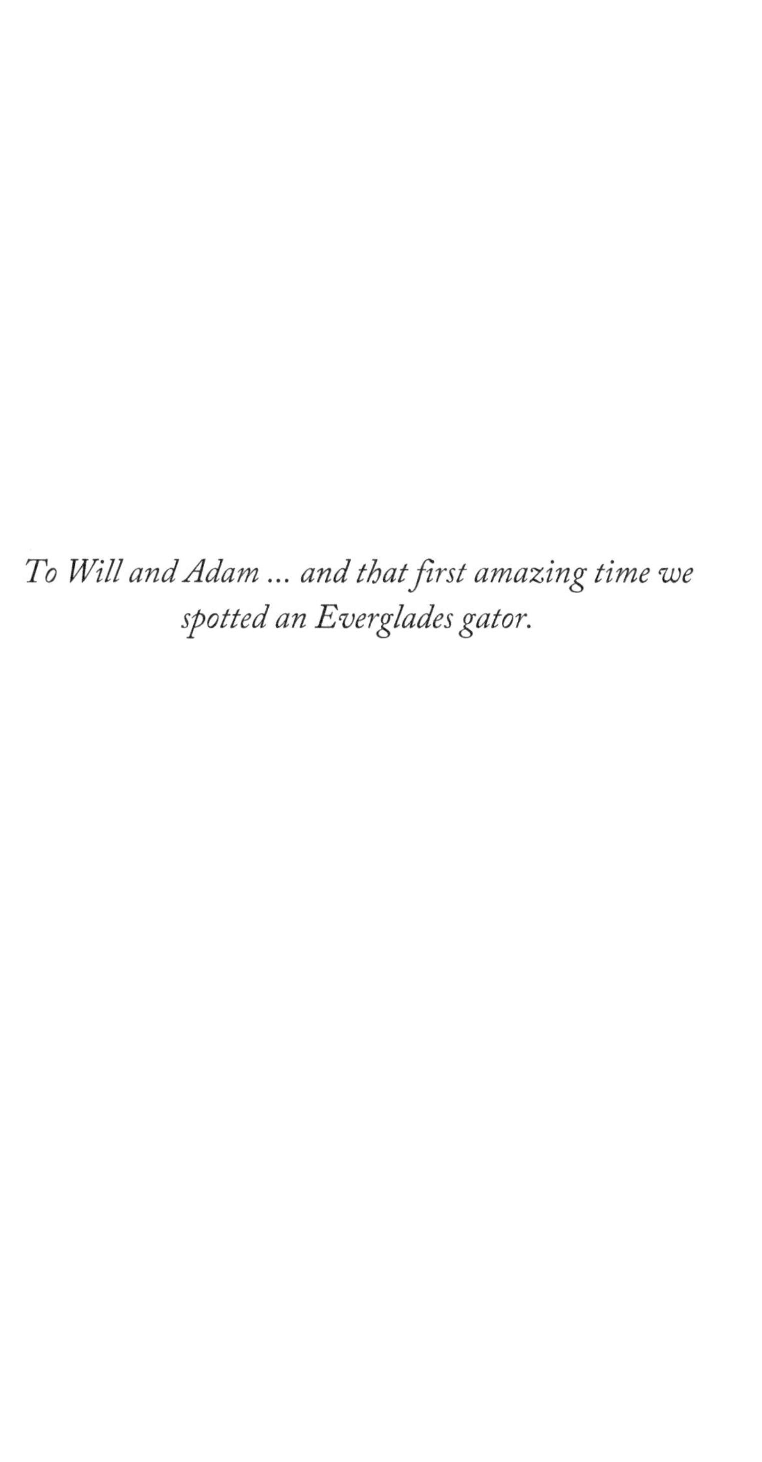

To Will and Adam ... and that first amazing time we spotted an Everglades gator.

There are no other Everglades in the world.

— Marjorie Stoneman Douglas

What is man without the beasts?

If all the beasts were gone,

Man would die from a great loneliness of spirit.

For whatever happens to the beasts,

Soon happens to man.

All things are connected.

— Chief Seattle, Suquamish and Duwamish, 1855

TABLE OF CONTENTS

PROLOGUE

Sydney crouched, hardly daring to breathe. The poacher was right here! Her heart thumped so loud, she felt sure he'd hear it.

"You kids shouldn't be running around the swamplands like this," he said. "It's dangerous."

Yeah right, Sydney thought, so I gathered.

"Come on out. You need help. There's a monster alligator has his pad right down the bank a few yards away from here. They're territorial, you know. And you're like meat in his pantry. He'll be able to smell you."

Another branch snapped. He was so close.

"Come on out." The man spoke sweetly now, just your nice, friendly neighborhood poacher. "You're much too young to be out here alone. We can go back to my shack and have something hot to eat. Soup, or something. I bet you're hungry. Then I'll fly you out of here in my helicopter. You'll be back home before you know it. And then you can bring help for your friends. There are a few of you out here, aren't there? I'm sure your parents must be worried."

Hot tears trickled down Sydney's cheeks. Yes, she knew her parents would be worried. But this man wouldn't help her. Her head spun. Maybe he would. He sounded quite nice. Maybe he wasn't one of the poachers. Maybe he was just someone who lived here in the swamp. For a minute, she almost stood up—almost ran to him.

Then common sense took over. This man was bad. All he wanted was to get rid of her so she wouldn't mess up his animal poaching business.

"I won't hurt you," the man said. "I promise."

No. Leave me alone. Get away from me. I hope an alligator eats you, you creep.

"I can see you right there."

Could he see her? No. If he could, he'd have grabbed her. Trembling, she forced herself to stay motionless. Sweat trickled down her forehead, into her eyes and down her cheeks.

The man was moving away, banging a stick or something at the bushes. He didn't know where she was! Sydney dared a shallow breath.

"Hey!"

There he was again!

"It's a rush being in the Glades in the dark, isn't it?"

He chuckled. "All those gators. There are thousands of them, you know. Big-toothed lizards, and some of them four hundred pounds! Ever see their eyes at night? Red. Real slit-eyed and mean. Hungry. And the way they lie there, their eyes just above the water, watching, waiting. Threw my dad's dog into the swamp once—right next to a humongous one—but the dumb dog got away. Never saw a dog swim so fast."

Sydney shivered. Silence again. Had he gone? Thank you, God! But what about the alligators? A gunshot rang in the distance. The man swore and muttered something to himself. When he spoke again, he sounded angry. "Bet that big gator is sniffing for you right now," he said. "Serve you right if it grabs you and drags you under and takes you on a nice-old death roll. That's what you kids are asking for—looking for trouble, snooping around in the swamplands."

For a moment she almost told him she wasn't snooping around in the swamplands. He could have the swamplands. All she wanted to do was go home.

CHAPTER I

Thunderheads loomed. The long saw grass swayed and shivered in the wind. Megan stood at the cabin door and stared out at the roiling waters of Florida Bay. A maze of canals snaked into the surrounding swampland and into the wild—a scary place with monster alligators everywhere. She was longing to go there. Adam, the cute guy she'd met at the campground store last night, would be helping his park ranger uncle on the airboat ride at 5:00 p.m. It was almost five o'clock now.

She glanced over at her family. Her parents lounged on the patio sofa, reading. Sydney, her twin sister, clicked away at her iPhone. Luke, her ten-year-old brother, was destroying zombies in some *Walking Dead* video game. In the distance, thunder rolled. A storm was heading right toward them. There was no way her parents would let her go on the airboat. It was much better not to ask and then apologize later.

Megan walked into the bathroom. She pulled on a faded black T-shirt and skinny jeans and ran a brush through her long, dark hair. Then, as quietly as possible, she removed the window screen, climbed out the window, and headed off toward the boat dock. She was going to go into those swamplands or die trying.

The sound of guitar music came from the boathouse. Great! Sounded like Adam was there. Running to avoid the dive-bombing mosquitoes, she opened the shed door and peeked in.

Adam, tall and slim, dark ponytail held loosely with a braided leather band and wearing a long-sleeved white T-shirt and cutoff blue jeans, ran his fingers through a final chord of Hendrix's *Voodoo Child* and looked up, smiling. "Wassup?"

"Not much." Megan smiled. "Any chance I can go on the airboat ride at five?"

Adam shook his head. "My uncle canceled it. A storm's coming."

"Canceled it? Well, could you maybe take me?"

Adam shook his head apologetically. "I'll ask if he can fit you in tomorrow."

"But we're leaving tomorrow."

She smiled up at him. He seemed a little older than she was, probably a senior. She liked his high cheekbones and slightly slanted eyes. She'd never met a Miccosukee

Indian before. Last night she noticed Sydney watching him, too. He was way cute. His smooth guitar playing gave her goosebumps.

The shed door creaked open and Sydney appeared, followed by Luke. Sydney had changed into her new blue cambric shirt, tied in a knot above the waist, and Juicy Couture frayed denim shorts. Her long blonde hair fell in soft waves to her shoulders. Megan saw her chances with Adam disappearing fast.

"Mom says you can't go out on the airboat, Megs," Sydney said.

"You told her I was going, didn't you?"

Sydney shook her head. "Not even. Anyway, it's dangerous."

"Wimp."

Adam laughed. "I thought twins agreed about everything."

"Only on a few matters of life and death," Megan said.

"Are you guys really twins?" Adam studied the two girls with interest. "You look totally different. I guess you both have dark eyes, though."

"We're fraternal twins. Not identical." Sydney twisted her blonde hair into a knot on the top of her head. "She has blonde hair, too. She dyed it black to try to look like a Goth."

"No way are we identical." Megan touched her dark hair self-consciously, then looked out the window to the mysterious swamplands. How could she persuade Adam to take them out? She couldn't bear to come all the way to the Everglades and not see them up close! "Is it okay if I go sit on the airboat?" she said.

"Sure." Adam smiled. "Lots of mosquitoes out there, though."

Megan headed out the door. Stepping outside the boathouse was like stepping into an oven. For a moment, she regretted her decision. But what fun was sitting inside? She ran down the boat ramp. Climbing into the small airboat, she sat on the high driver's seat and looked around at the surrounding mangroves. The air was humid enough to wring and get water. Clouds of mosquitoes descended on her head. Everything smelled dank, funky.

If the boat were just a bit farther out from the dock, there'd be more to see, she thought. Maybe she'd even spot an alligator. She uncoiled the mooring line from the cleat and tied it, leaving a longer line so the boat could float out a bit. She was pleased with her sailor's knot. Girl Guides hadn't been a total waste of time.

Slowly, the boat drifted out. The air felt cooler. She stretched out and looked around, listening to the lapping water. Nice. Without warning, the boat spun round. Megan gasped. Oh no! The sailor's knot didn't work—the line was loose. She and the boat were heading out into Florida Bay. She jumped to her feet. "Adam!" she shouted. "Adam!"

Adam ran out of the shed. "Stay there! What happened?" He splashed through the muddy flats and into the deeper water and caught hold of the boat. Climbing into the driver's seat, he grabbed the wheel.

Sydney splashed through the water and tumbled into

the back of the boat, followed by Luke. Sopping wet, Luke looked around, beaming. "Cool boat! I've never been in an airboat. Can we go for just a short spin, Adam? Please!"

Great, Luke was backing her up. Megan looked imploringly at Adam. "Please! And I'm sorry about the mooring line."

"Okay, okay," Adam checked the brooding clouds. "We'll go for just a short run, ten minutes max. That storm's coming fast."

"Cool." Megan beamed as she curled her long legs under her body and settled into a front seat.

"Hold on." Adam turned the wheel.

The propeller fan roared and the airboat headed across the bay toward the dark Everglades.

CHAPTER 2

Grass marshlands shimmered in all directions. Megan's dark eyes sparkled as the boat skimmed across the choppy water, heading for the distant mangrove islands. Cypress trees, draped with shrouds of gray hanging moss, looked just as she'd pictured them. She imagined Dracula flying above, silhouetted black against the slate-gray sky. Mangrove trees with spooky, twisted roots lined the banks. What a deliciously creepy place! So gothic! She could smell a million plants growing and another million rotting. "Where are the alligators?" she said. "I'd just love to see one."

"Oh yeah! Cool!" Luke grinned.

"They hang out in the mangroves." Adam executed a 360-degree turn into the shallows and turned off the engine, pointing at the high-rooted mangrove trees. "Watch for a while and you're sure to spot a few." Without the roar of the engine, everything was still. Luke leaned over and dangled a hand in the black water.

"Careful," Adam warned. "Keep your hands in the boat. We have fifteen-foot-long alligators here. They're killing machines. They'd love to get a hold of you for lunch. Look back there; there's a big, hungry dude checking us out."

Megan stared at the scaly-skinned creature lazing in the shallows. "Ooh, I want to see it close-up. Can you get it to come over here?"

"My uncle has some marshmallows for them." Adam opened the lid of a bench seat and took out a packet. "Here, alligator. Try some of these."

The white marshmallows bobbed up and down on the top of the brown water. Sydney laughed. "Marshmallows! Why would an alligator eat marshmallows?"

"I guess they eat just about anything. My uncle doesn't want to throw bloody meat into the creek."

"I suppose." Megan stared, fascinated as the prehistoric-looking creature came closer. It opened its mouth wide, showing sharp, pointed teeth, and gulped down the marshmallows.

"Seems sort of mean to feed them marshmallows. What if they get a toothache or something?" Sydney leaned over the side of the boat. "Hullo, alligator." Without warning, the alligator thrashed its tail, whamming it down on the water. Sydney yelped and leaped back. The alligator stared at her with cold, hooded eyes. Face pale, Sydney wiped off drops of muddy water.

Taking a quick look at the darkening sky, Adam started the engine. The noise of the boat flushed out cormorants and great white herons. Spray flew and wind whipped their hair. Sydney gripped the handrails, and Luke hung on to his L.A. Angels baseball cap. Megan stretched her arms high, pretending she was on a roller coaster.

The storm hit. Lightning streaked the sky. Thunder boomed. Swollen clouds spat single, hard drops of water and then opened. Rain poured down in torrents.

Sydney crouched, covering her head with her hands. Luke pulled his black baseball cap down as far as it would go, slipped his Gameboy under his damp khaki T-shirt, and huddled up next to Sydney, shivering.

Gusts of wind churned the bay into a boiling mass of waves that rocked and shook the airboat. Adam slowed down. Wiping the rain out of his eyes, he peered through the gray water-world. "We've got to get to shore. It's too open here. This lightning's right on us."

Bumping up and down through the choppy water, they headed for the edge of the bay and turned into a maze of winding channels lined with mangrove trees. The boat rocked as it collided with mangrove roots and protruding cypress knees. Hands clenched on the wheel, Adam maneuvered through the narrows, looking for a safe place to stop. Lightning clawed the sky and hit the water.

Adam pumped up the speed. The canal widened and he roared down it.

An ominous clap of thunder shook the air.

"We have to get away from the water!" Megan jumped up, reached across Adam, and grabbed the steering. The boat veered to the left.

"Watch out!" Too late, Adam grabbed back the wheel. With a loud thud, the airboat plowed into a mud bank. Megan stared in dismay. She'd screwed up this time.

"Look at the boat!" Frowning, Adam tried to start the motor. Churning, the propeller spun round in the mud. "We're stuck."

They certainly did seem to be stuck. Megan hoped it wasn't as bad as it seemed. "We'll push it out of the mud as soon as it stops raining. Let's get away from this lightning!" She scrambled across the seat and jumped into the muddy creek. Wet branches whacked her face as she splashed to shore, hopping around the tangled mangrove roots and cypress knees. Behind her, she could hear Sydney whimpering. It doesn't take much to make Sydney whimper anyway, she thought, though I feel a bit like whimpering myself.

Again, forked lightning zapped the water, followed by loud claps of thunder. She took a quick, nervous look at the sky. Was it true that if the thunder closely followed the lightning, then the lightning was dangerously nearby? Was it true that if you heard the thunder, it meant you'd survived the lightning? Did lightning travel across water? She slipped, gasping as her sneakers caught in a mangrove root and her ankle twisted.

She plunged ahead, finding it easier not to watch

where she was going and not to think about consequences. Adam, Sydney, and Luke followed through the snarl of branches, vines, and spiderwebs.

After five minutes, Adam stopped and pointed to a limestone outcrop. "Let's get under there. Watch where you put your hands, and look out for snakes and spiders."

Ducking under the ledge, they huddled together, shivering. Rain dripped from their shirts and jeans. The storm beat down on their shelter. A waterfall of rain poured from the ledge above, splashing onto the saturated ground. The thunder sounded ever louder, like a freight train rumbling over them. Luke shivered and brushed his dripping hair out of his eyes. Sydney began to cry quietly, wiping the tears from her wet face.

Adam stared out into the wet. "Looks like we'll be spending the night."

"Not good. That's when the animals come out," Luke said.

"What animals?" Sydney moved closer to Adam.

"Just rattlesnakes, pythons, alligators, bobcats, black bears, and the occasional panther," Megan said. "All looking for a snack."

Luke leaned forward, blue eyes wide. "Have you heard of goat suckers?"

"No, what are they?" Sydney sounded as if she'd rather not know.

"I read about them a few months ago," Luke said. "They're animals with fangs and red eyes."

Megan laughed. "That's so junk."

"It's true," Luke said. "They've been found in South America or Mexico, I can't remember which. And farmers saw signs of them here in Florida."

"What signs?"

"Goats and chickens with their blood all sucked out." Luke pulled a finger across his throat. "That's why they're called goat suckers." He moved closer to Sydney. "What time is it?"

"Six. It'll be dark soon."

"Try to get some sleep," Adam said.

Close by, something shrieked. Megan shivered. It was hunt or be hunted out there.

She stared out into the thousands of gathering shadows.

CHAPTER 3

Lightning descended like a spear for a huge mahogany tree. Stunned, Megan watched as the trunk cracked and split. Smoldering branches crashed into the creek. I hope that didn't land on the boat, she thought, glancing at Adam. He had his eyes closed and didn't seem to have noticed. She decided not to tell him. There was nothing they could do about it, anyway.

The noises of the Everglades surrounded them. Animals hooted and shrieked. Wind wailed and branches squeaked. The river gurgled. Close by she could hear the cracking and rustling of something pulling itself through the bushes. Maybe they were right in the alligators' path. She shivered. Uncomfortable in her wet clothes, she wrapped her arms around her legs and listened miserably to the sounds of the swamp.

Luke broke the heavy silence. "Have you ever seen a rattler? I saw a photo of one once. They're huge six-foot monsters with big heads and purplish-gray bodies. They have sort of diamond crisscross markings. The most dangerous snakes in North America. Brimming over with venom."

"Don't talk about snakes, Luke," Sydney said.

"There's probably one nesting right under my butt," Luke groaned.

"Stop thinking about it, Luke!" Her wet jeans squishing, Megan curled up with her arm under her head.

"I'm really thirsty. And hungry. Are we going soon?"

Megan groaned. "Just try to get some sleep."

The downpour stopped suddenly. Rain dripped from the ledge. Sydney nudged Adam. "Look at that red moon rising."

"It's called a hunter's moon," Adam said.

"Looks like a jack-o'-lantern," Megan said. "Be great for Halloween."

"Halloween in the Glades would be cool," Luke said, pushing his tangled brown hair out of his eyes. "I could go as a swamp zombie."

Sydney scratched her legs and groaned. "These mosquitoes think I'm a Slurpee."

"Try this." Adam scooped a handful of mud from the wet in front of the shelter.

"You want me to smear that on?" Sydney looked dubious.

"Sure. Mosquitoes won't bite through it."

Sydney stuck her finger into the mud and circled her eyes and cheeks. She turned to Megan. "How do I look?"

Megan peered at her and giggled. "Interesting camo paint. Wild. Give me some too."

"It's the Miccosukee version of DEET," Adam said. He smeared mud on his arms.

"Have you always lived here?" Sydney said.

Adam shook his head. "I grew up in Miami; my mom's family was from there. My dad was a Miccosukee Indian. The Indians moved to the Glades to get away from the Spanish settlers. That was long ago, when my great-grandparents were young."

"How could they have lived here? What did they eat?"

"Wish I'd asked." Adam curled up in the corner and looked into the night. "My grandfather told me stories about the first people who lived here."

"What about?"

"Usually about people who got into trouble. Like the guy who is hunting alone in the swamplands and falls into a hole and twists his ankle. That twisted ankle is the end of him. I used to think my grandfather wanted to scare me, but I think he was warning me to be careful. Out here, a small mistake is as bad as a bullet in your head."

CHAPTER 4

Morning arrived hot and damp. Megan woke and sat up, scratching and slapping as she looked around the cave. "Look at the beetles! There are just hundreds. Oh, this is so gross! I'm out of here."

"Watch for snakes," Adam said. "They come out after the rain."

"I need to find a tree," Sydney said. "Will you come with me, Megs?"

"Don't be a baby. Go by yourself."

"Please. You know you have to go, too."

Megan shrugged. "Oh, okay, come on."

"Adam, will you go with me?" Luke said.

"Sure, dude, let's go."

Adam and Luke crawled out of the shelter and made

their way behind the nearest bush. Sydney started sloshing through the mud to a high rock mound, with Megan following. Sydney shrieked.

"Don't scream like that!" Megan said. "You freaked me out." Then she stared, horrified. Snakes! The mound was covered with snakes twined around each other like balls of different-colored rope. Snakes of all colors, some big, some small, some black and thin, some fat and glossy gray, some striped and orange and quite beautiful in their own weird way.

"You're right about the snakes, Adam," she shouted.

Luke charged out from behind the bush. "Where? Where?"

Megan pointed at the mound.

"Oh, wow!"

"Just don't go near them," Adam said. "They're warming up after the rain."

"You're not scared of them?"

"'Course I'm scared of them. I hate snakes. But they won't bite you unless you step on them or scare them or something."

Luke pointed. "Look at that sucker!" A fat green python lay curled, taking up the top of a large granite rock. With half-closed yellow eyes, he watched them as he moved lazily, muscles rippling. "Boy, he could really crush you," Luke said. "He must be twelve feet long. There're more than 30,000 pythons in the Glades. I saw it on TV."

"How could there be?" Megan said. "I don't think pythons even come from Florida."

"They were pets," Luke said.

"No way."

"Way. People let them out in the wild when they get too big for their tanks."

"You should stay away from that mound, anyway," Adam said. "It's a burial mound. See, it's covered with shells."

"Omigod. Don't tell me the place is haunted, too," Sydney said. "You mean there's skeletons under there and stuff?"

Adam shook his head. "Even if it was haunted, they'd be friendly ghosts. They'd be the ghosts of the Miccosukee. Anyway, let's get the boat and go."

"But are there skeletons?" Sydney said.

"He said it's a burial mound, didn't he?" Megan said. She turned to Adam. "I'm on my way."

Megan slid down the bank, keeping a close watch on where she put her hands and feet. What a creepy place this was turning out to be. Snakes! Ghosts! She couldn't wait to get back on the boat and get out of here. Where had they left it? She looked up and down the bank. No sign of the boat. With a horrible feeling of misgiving, she moved closer to the water and spotted charred wood and a patch of blue paint showing under the branches of a huge fallen tree. Oh no! That burning tree had landed on the boat and nuked it.

"Adam!" she shouted. "Something's happened to the boat!"

Adam jumped down the bank in four leaps, landing

at her side. "My uncle's going to kill me."

Branches and burned leaves covered the bright blue wood of the half-submerged airboat. A twisted propeller blade stuck out from the mud.

"Now what?" Luke said. "How will we get out of here?"

Megan felt a pang of guilt. "Mom and Dad will call the park rangers." She took Luke's hand. "And Adam's uncle is a park ranger. If we stay near the boat, they'll find us. We'll be fine."

Adam glanced at the looming storm clouds. "There's another storm coming. We need a better shelter. There's no way we're going to get out of here soon."

"We can live without food for days, but we need lots of water in this heat," Sydney said.

"I read a way people can drink their pee, but I don't really remember it." Luke frowned, his face wrinkled in concentration. "You dig a hole and cover it with plastic or something, and the pee sort of evaporates up and water drops slide down. You need a cup in the hole to catch the water. We could try it."

Megan rolled her eyes. "Omigod, Luke! There is no way I'm going to drink pee no matter what you do to it. I'd rather die of thirst."

"Well, okay," Luke thought for a moment. "We could tie our shirts around our ankles and walk around in the morning and collect dew and then wring out the water."

"I'm starving," Sydney said. "Are there any of those alligator marshmallows left?"

"Yeah." Adam nodded. "Why didn't I think of that? My uncle takes stuff for the tourists on swamp trips."

Wading into the water, he pulled branches away from part of the burnt storage seat. He forced the covering of a storage locker open and pulled out a small ice chest. "Oatmeal cookies and a six-pack of Cokes. Yes! Marshmallows and some other stuff." As he burrowed into the storage locker, he pulled out and waved his finds: a canvas sheet and six plastic rain jackets. With his haul clutched to his chest, he waved a can of insect repellent.

"Ooh, give me some of that!" Megan ran forward and grabbed the can of DEET. The packet of cookies slid out of Adam's grasp and splashed into the muddy river.

"No!" Adam plunged in after it, groping in the mud. "That's the end of the cookies."

Megan's face turned red.

Luke opened the packet and groaned. "They're soaked."

"We can't eat them now—that swamp stuff will make us sick," Sydney said. She glared at Megan.

"It's just water." Defiantly, Megan bit into a cookie, grimaced, and swallowed it fast. "Tastes fine."

Adam passed around the plastic jackets and handed Sydney the insect repellent. "Okay, if we have to spend another night, let's find a better shelter. We need to make it close to the boat so anyone looking can find us."

They pulled their way up the bank again, past the limestone outcrop where they'd spent the night, and up onto a flat granite platform.

Megan reached the top first. She stood and looked around. "We're surrounded by swamp and water. Not much else out there. Never mind. Soon, we'll probably see the park rangers sloshing their way toward us."

"Do you think so?" Sydney looked hopeful.

"Of course," Megan nodded. "They're probably preparing the rescue team right now. Tonight, we could even be on the local news. Even CNN or something. 'Teens Survive Terrible Night in the Glades.'"

"What about 'Teens Don't Survive Terrible Night in the Glades'?" Sydney muttered.

"No one even knows we took the boat," Adam said. "My uncle won't be returning from Key West until Monday. What about your mom and dad? Did you tell them where you were going?"

Megan shook her head. "No. They'll have no idea where we are. Mom will be reaching that frantic stage. But she'll do something. She's a Marine. She'll work it out."

"How?" Sydney muttered.

Megan felt hot tears welling up in her eyes.

"Come on, let's build the shelter," Adam said. "Up here looks like the best place, so we can see if anybody's coming."

Poking around at the base of the platform, Adam pulled away a clump of ferns, revealing a four-foot-wide opening about a foot in height at the left end and two or three feet at the right. "What about here?"

With a stick, he began digging the crumbling limestone rocks and sand, opening up a dark, musty hole.

"There's a cave of some sort. It goes quite a ways back. It's high enough to sit in, and we'll be dry at night."

Megan crawled in, followed by Luke and Sydney.

"Watch for snakes and spiders," Adam said. "And go easy on those Cokes. They may be all we have for a while."

Megan looked wistfully at the dripping packet of cookies. Those would have been good right about now.

CHAPTER 5

When she'd finished her share of a Coke, Megan jumped up. "If we follow the river, maybe we'll find someone. When I saw the survivor guy in the Everglades on TV, he found a fence and a freeway running right by where he was."

Sydney frowned. "I thought you said we should stay with the boat?"

"Well, you can stay," Megan said. "I'm going to explore."

She headed off along the bank, stamping through mud and rotten vegetation. Adam and Luke followed. Sydney tied one of the plastic raincoats around her waist as a skirt and ran to catch up.

Adam stopped, scraped some small oysters off the nearest mangrove root, and offered one to Sydney.

Sydney nibbled the smallest section possible. "It tastes good, Adam."

"It's alive, you know," Megan said.

"No, it's not."

"Yes, it is. Until you bit it, that is."

Adam laughed. "Don't worry, Sydney. Oysters are good for you, dead or alive."

"Yuck, there's a little living oyster creeping down your throat," Megan said. "Help, help, let me out of here. Oh no, I'm in the stomach and the stomach acid's getting me."

"Shut up!" Sydney shouted. "I'm starved and scratched and thirsty and filthy. Maybe we'll never find our way out of here. We'll end up starving and our bodies will be torn apart and eaten by alligators."

"It's not that bad," Megan said. "It's beautiful here . . . in a weird way." She looked down and smiled as small red frogs popped in and out of the mud. A green heron waded by, and a small alligator with clay-colored eyes peeked out from the shallows.

Adam began leading the way, and she followed close behind him. He turned to her and pointed ahead. "There's a type of trail here, leading up the bank. Let's see what's up this way."

The jungle clamored around them. They stumbled through a grove of huge gumbo-limbo trees covered with gray lichen. Mud made each step difficult, and the air was hot and sticky. Sweat drenched their bodies. Adam picked up a sharp rock and scratched notches in tree trunks to mark their path back. When they reached the top of the rise, they were panting. Below, a silver ribbon of water gleamed between the dense foliage.

"We'll go down here," Adam said. "Hey! Look here!" He pushed his way into the bushes and came out carrying a round yellow fruit.

"What is it?"

"Grapefruit!"

"Can we eat it? Is it the regular sort of grapefruit we eat for breakfast?"

"Yeah. Indians must have planted trees here years ago."

Adam peeled the grapefruit and handed out the lemony segments. Megan took a mouthful and winced. The fruit was wonderfully juicy, but bitter. She licked her lips. "Are there any more?"

Adam shook his head. "Not on that tree, but we should keep looking. We might find something else. This trail must go somewhere."

Luke started down the slippery slope, followed by Megan. "Something smells gross," he said, slapping buzzing flies away from his face.

"Probably you," Megan said.

"Did you bring the DEET?"

Megan shook her head.

Luke pulled his Walkman out of his pocket. He plugged his ears and turned up the volume. "What? Can't hear you." He ran forward and stepped on a slick rock. He slid, tried to regain his balance, and then began sliding down the slope, crashing into a big hole.

"Luke!" Megan ran forward. Luke lay on his back in

a slough hole about eight feet deep that had been ripped out of the limestone earth by a fallen gumbo-limbo tree. The whole place stank. Flies swarmed.

"Adam!" Megan screamed.

Adam jumped feetfirst into the hole and pulled Luke up into a sitting position. "Are you okay? Can you climb out?"

"Yeah." Luke's face was pale, and he clutched his arm.

Megan stared. Something was moving in the far corner of the hole. "Adam!" she shrieked. "Over there! Behind Luke. What's that?"

Adam stepped forward cautiously. Megan ran around the edge of the hole and leaned over to get a better view. Then she screamed. Three dead monkeys with blank, vacant eyes lay twisted on the ground, smothered by a seething mass of flies.

"We've got to get away from here," she shouted.

"Let's go." Turning away, Adam stumbled down the trail.

"But monkeys don't live in the Glades, do they?"

"No."

"So how did they get here?"

Adam retched and shook his head.

Megan stared back at the hole. "Is it an animal trap?"

"Let's just move on." Adam headed off down the trail and Megan, Sydney, and Luke followed in a line, trying to stay close together.

Sydney put her hand on Luke's shoulder. "Did you hurt your hand?"

"It's just a bit twisted."

"You're lucky it's not cut," Megan said. "That place was gross." She came to an abrupt stop and pointed through the trees to a clearing. "We've got neighbors."

"Oh wow!" Sydney beamed with relief.

"Wait. Be careful." Adam spoke softly. "Let's check them out before they see us."

Cautiously, Adam and Megan approached the shack.

CHAPTER 6

The wooden shack was perched on a three-foot-high base of thick limestone bricks. The solid-looking door was locked with a thick chain, and the windows were high and narrow. Adam got a toehold on the limestone bricks, climbed up, and peered inside, trying to make out shapes in the gloom. "There doesn't seem to be anyone in there. Looks like Dracula's pad."

"What do you mean?" Megan whispered.

"Place is full of cages. Must be a poacher's shack."

"Maybe they've left some food. And water." Megan walked to the door and knocked hard, waited a minute then pushed it, jangling the handle. "Anybody home?"

"Let's try the windows."

Silently, they walked around the house, pushing at

the frames.

"Here!" Adam pushed hard, and a small window slid up. "Can you get through here?"

"Yeah," Megan said. "I'm used to climbing out of real small bedroom windows. Help me up."

Adam crouched down, and Megan stepped on his back and slid in through the window. Sliding her legs down, she balanced on the top of a toilet cistern and sprang to the floor, then tiptoed from the bathroom toward the living room. What if there's someone here? She thought. I bet they wouldn't be friendly. They'd be bad dudes. I don't want to be here. Her heart pumped faster. She forced herself to walk forward. Even before she went through the living room door, the smell filled her nostrils: rancid and rank, so strong she could taste it. She froze as she heard squawking and weird screeching and stared around, eyes wide with horror.

Piles of alligator skins, deer hide, and furry pelts covered a long table against the far wall. Crates of skins stood in corners. Boxes of skulls gleamed white. Knives, pistols, and sharp-edged machetes lay on the floor. Metal cages glistened in the dim light, and the air reeked of straw and urine. Megan stared at the nearest cage. Something moved. She jumped back. There were living animals here, too.

Scanning the room from side to side, she ran to the front door and pulled back the bolt. The door opened slightly, then stuck.

"It's chained," Adam called. "Open a bigger window."

"You won't believe this place." Megan pushed the lock

of a larger window, and Adam and Luke climbed through. Sydney stayed outside, peering in.

"Oh, gross!" Luke grimaced as the rank stench hit him. "What's that smell? Smells like blood."

"Poachers," Adam said, staring around the room. "See the animals in the cages, the animal skins?"

As Megan's eyes grew accustomed to the gloom, she saw some of the cages held birds, beautiful birds with blue and red plumage, and a group of small, round-eyed owls that stared solemnly at her. Other cages held turtles, tortoises, red and green tree frogs, and bearded dragons. Two small marmosets crouched in the corner of a cage, looking sick and frightened. A fairylike Key deer, with big Bambi eyes, watched nervously.

Luke grabbed Adam's arm. "There's someone in there!"

Adam whirled around. A childlike shape stood behind the bars of a small cage.

"Oh no!" Megan ran to the cage. A small animal with wild orange hair held out its arms to her, making a distressed peeping sound. "It's a baby orangutan!"

Adam shook his head. "These creeps are more than local poachers; they're into the big time. They're smuggling animals from South America and Borneo. Rare animals, endangered species."

Its small fingers pushing through the bars, the orangutan reached for Megan's hand, pulled it up to its mouth, and sucked her thumb.

"Oh, poor baby," she cried. "He still needs his mother to feed him." The little animal looked at her with sad, wise eyes. "We've got to get him out of here."

"*We* have to get out of this place," Sydney said. "We have to save ourselves. Then we can come back and save the animals."

Adam nodded. "The poachers could come back at any time. They won't want any witnesses. We have to go."

"Let's see if there's any food first." Megan turned and headed in the direction of what she thought must be the kitchen.

"I want to get away from here!" Sydney's voice sounded frantic. "We don't want to eat their disgusting food."

"I do. I'm starving," Luke said.

Megan gave the baby orangutan a parting pat. "I'll be back, Baby Furball. I promise."

They ran into the small, dark kitchen. Flies buzzed and bugs crawled in a big sink full of dried blood. A shelf held cans, crackers, coffee, and powdered milk, and they packed a few cans of soup into a plastic bag. Luke whooped when he found two plastic bottles of water.

Megan took the orangutan a cracker. He looked at it, sniffed it, and put it behind his ear. "Oh dear, Baby, you're supposed to eat it." Megan sighed. She ran back to the others. "That poor little guy. He isn't going to live if we don't get him to a vet who knows how to feed him."

"The poachers will try to feed him," Adam said. "He's worth big bucks."

Megan was last when they left the shack, smiling sadly at the small orangutan as she closed the door. The four made their way through the jungle and reached their makeshift shelter. Looking pleased with himself, Luke produced a can opener he'd grabbed as they left the kitchen.

"You're the man!" Adam said, giving him a high five.

They opened two cans of chicken noodle soup and took turns gulping the contents. The jungle was silent in the afternoon heat.

Adam pulled his damp T-shirt over his head and hung it on a bush. Megan gasped. Adam's back was crisscrossed with white, lumpy scars.

"What happened to your back?" she said. She immediately wished she hadn't said anything, but it was out now. Both Sydney and Luke stared at Adam.

"Burned."

"How?" Luke stood up to get a closer look. "Were you in a fire?"

"Yeah, in Miami. Our house burned down."

"So you didn't get out in time?"

"I did. But I went back in to get my dog."

"Oh!" Megan stared in admiration. "Did you manage to save him?"

"Yeah."

"That's so great, Adam."

"It wasn't, really. My dad died. I didn't know he was home."

"Oh." Megan swallowed hard.

"I thought he was still at the pub. I should have saved him."

Their faces solemn, Megan and Luke exchanged glances. Sydney, with tears in her eyes, stared at Adam and then frowned at Megan. Megan looked away. She felt bad enough already. How was she supposed to have known some awful thing like that had happened? She wondered why Adam's dad hadn't managed to leave the house. And what about his mom? She didn't dare ask. So Adam had lived most of his life in Miami and not in the Indian reservation. That must be why he didn't seem to know much about surviving in the Everglades. Scary, as the rest of them knew nothing at all.

CHAPTER 7

Megan woke as dawn crept into the tent. She lay wedged between Sydney and Luke, her legs entwined with theirs. Her right arm was numb and all of her scratches and bites throbbed. Just thinking about them made them all itch. Stop it, she thought, thinking about itches makes them worse. She sat up and looked around her. Everyone else was sound asleep, their faces flushed from the steamy heat and patterned with crisscross lines of ferns, twigs, and dirt.

She wiggled forward and crawled outside. The Glades looked cool and beautiful in the dawn light. As she sipped some water from the bottle, she thought about the baby orangutan. How frightened and confused he must be—one moment swinging in the trees and the next taken from his tree home and locked up.

Poor, little baby orangutan. He was so young; he could never take care of himself. Could he even eat by himself? I'm going to try to feed him, she decided. Maybe I can dip my finger in some powdered milk and feed him like I fed my little orphaned kittens.

She peeked back into the shelter. Everyone was still asleep. Quick and silent, she made her way along the bank and into the wilderness toward the poacher's shack. Ghostlike gray moss brushed her hair, and the sticky silver strands of spiderwebs clung to her face. She shook her hair hard to remove any spiders and began to hum the Marines' song. She figured a power-packed song would make her feel better. After all, the Marines went through much worse than this all the time. They wouldn't even notice spiders' webs.

A dark shadow fluttered overhead, and with nasty thoughts of vampire bats, she looked up. An anhinga bird sat in the branches of a tall palm tree, spreading its wings out to dry. Megan laughed. It looked so odd, like a Dr. Seuss bird. She wished she were just a happy visitor in the Glades. Perhaps she would be soon. They'd probably be rescued that afternoon. Someone would come looking for them by then. Adam's uncle would notice the boat was missing. He'd get back from work early, and he'd sound the alarm. They'd send motorboats. Perhaps they'd send rescue helicopters. That would be even faster. She scanned the overcast sky.

At the poacher's shack, nothing had changed. Megan

stood in the jungle for a while and watched. There was no sign of the poachers. Going inside the shack was risky, she knew. Poachers were nasty people. They had no worries about killing animals for money. They might feel the same way about a girl who was a threat to them. Her heart started beating faster. What she was about to do was dangerous, but she decided to do it anyway. She cared about the baby orangutan.

She pulled an empty gas can to the window, jumped up on it, and climbed inside. Nancy Drew, girl detective, that's me, she thought. Motionless, she looked around and listened. No poachers. Her heart still beat fast, though. She took a deep breath, trying to calm down. Stop worrying! she told herself. You're getting as wussy as Sydney. She tiptoed to the living room door. As they saw her, the birds in the cages began screeching, and the little monkeys jabbered and flung themselves around the bars.

Megan ran straight to the little orangutan. The small animal huddled at the back of the cage. When it saw Megan, it began cheeping, shaking the bars and squeezing its funny, worried-looking, little face up against them. "Baby," she whispered. "Look, Baby, I'm back. See, I've come back for you." Suddenly, she thought of her Marine mom, and how the Marines never left anyone behind. How she wished her mom were here, right now, to help. And her dad wouldn't be bad, either. They could always use a medic. But then she thought of trying to explain to her parents what she was doing. Well, actually, Mom, I'm in the pad of some really nasty men who smuggle and kill rare animals. No, Mom, I haven't a clue where the men are at the moment. Probably in the jungle somewhere with their big black guns, hunting. Yeah, I know they could come back at any time. No, I don't know what they would do to me. Yada, yada, yada. Maybe thinking about her parents wasn't such a bright idea.

The orangutan reached out and twisted its fingers into Megan's hair.

"Oh, Baby Furball, you're so sweet," Megan said. "Wait a minute. I'm going to find something for you to eat." She gently untwined his fingers and headed for the kitchen. A packet of powdered milk stood on the shelf. She mixed some of the powder with water.

There was a clanging sound. Megan whirled around. What was that? The sound came from the living room. Omigod. The poachers! That sounded like the chain on the door. They'd see the window was open. They'd know someone was inside. Frantic, her heart pounding, she looked for somewhere to hide. The only way out of the house was through the living room window. She was stuck. She dived behind the door and stood there, trembling. She knew there was every chance the poachers would kill her. What they were doing was highly illegal and highly remunerative. They wouldn't want witnesses. There was no way they would simply let her leave or help her and the others. It would be easy, much too easy, to get rid of her. She'd read of bodies being dumped into the Everglades' swamps. No one ever saw them again. Alligators ate every scrap. Her head reeled with fear.

She waited, not daring to breathe. Then she heard creaking. Was someone walking across the floor? If they came into the kitchen, they'd find her. Frantic, she looked around for a weapon. All she could see was a broom. Quickly she left her hiding place, grabbed the broom, and darted behind the door again. Except for the animal noises, everything was silent. After what seemed like an hour, she tiptoed out into the hallway and peeked into the living room. There was no one there. She'd been given another chance, but she was scared now. This was a dumb thing to do. She shouldn't be here. But how could she possibly leave without feeding the baby animal?

She took the mug of milk back to the cage. Dipping her finger into the mixture, she offered it to the little orangutan. First, he licked tentatively at the mixture; then he twined his hand in her hair again and began sucking. Again and again she dipped her fingers in the milk. The orangutan was really hungry, and he obviously enjoyed sucking. She wished he would hurry, but she had no way to tell him. And she was so glad he was eating.

She wondered where he came from. Not from the Everglades, that was for sure. There were no orangutans in Florida. He'd been brought in by the poachers, perhaps from as far away as Borneo or Africa. Running her fingers softly over his red hair, she pictured him in the jungle with his mom, cruising a treetop world, his little face happy and carefree. How awful for him to be captured, to be kept in a cage.

She was so glad to see him eating now, accepting her,

and even snuggling up to her. As the minutes went past, she forgot the horror of the room. She forgot about the poachers. She felt warm and protective of her new baby. Time stood still. The birds and creatures in the other cages watched her, all silent.

The sound of a loud engine broke the spell. Rotor blades chopped the sky. She jumped up. A rescue helicopter! She knew Mom would find her! Mom was a Marine. You could count on the Marines. The baby orangutan sprang back. Megan ran to the window and peered outside. The helicopter flew in low circles, preparing to land somewhere out of her sight. In the quiet, the whirr of the blades seemed amplified, the sound echoing off trees and water. Leaves whirled in the man-made gale, and a flock of herons soared into the air.

At the window, Megan froze. What if it wasn't the rescuers? What if it was the poachers? She had to get out of the house—fast. Scrambling out the window, she dropped to the ground, scraping her knees on the stones. She ran to the surrounding jungle and slid under some bushes, where she huddled, motionless.

Two men came single file up a trail from the water, making their way toward the house. Megan peeked through the bracken, a thrill of fright vibrating in her stomach. How would she know if these men were good or bad? They didn't look like they were a part of any search-and-rescue mission. They looked more like thugs. But that didn't mean they weren't a rescue team coming to rescue her. They could be nice, kind people, she thought. Mom always says you shouldn't judge people by appearances. She strained her ears to hear what they were saying.

The first man was thickset and unshaven, the sleeves of his army fatigues cut out to display thick muscles. "We can't afford to lose another orang; the boss will go berserk," he said, puffing as he climbed the trail. He had the same glossy black hair; dark, slanted eyes; and high cheekbones that Adam had, but his face was broad and coarse-looking. "Cost a packet getting the things from Borneo, and now four are dead. We have to get a vet before this one croaks on us, too."

"What vet? You can't get a freaking vet to come and treat trapped animals." The second man, thin and sharp-featured with stringy, long blond hair, wore a faded checked shirt and jeans with a nasty looking knife strapped on to his leg. Megan held her breath and burrowed deep into the grass. She could feel the electric buzz of fear. She knew who they were now. Please, God, don't let them find me, please, please, she prayed.

"Sure you can," the dark-haired man said. "Get anyone to do anything if you pay them enough."

At the house, they paused, wiping the sweat from their foreheads. "This place is the pits. Stinks. I told you not to kill stuff in here." The thin man struggled with the lock, muttering as he sorted through a set of keys. "Dude at the casino offered ten thousand bucks each for the Key deer."

"For Bambi? Thought they'd end up dried venison."

"There's a zoo hot for them. Dude says there's only about three hundred left in the world. The boss still wants to trap a panther. He's nuts. The Fish and Wildlife guys get seriously annoyed about trapped panthers."

Waiting until they'd walked into the shack and closed the door, Megan began to move as quietly as she could back along the trail. She pushed through the bushes, crouching, then stumbled and stifled a scream. A man stood in her path. The man, with tousled blond hair and deeply tanned skin, took off his designer sunglasses and stared at Megan. "What on Earth are you doing here?"

"Help me, please, help me," Megan swayed toward him. Wearing sun-bleached jeans and a white sweater, the guy was movie-star handsome. In fact, he looked like a young Leonardo DiCaprio. And he had the bluest eyes she'd ever seen. Relief washed over Megan. She had found help. And the help was pretty hot.

"What's wrong?"

"I'm lost here. My friends and I are all lost in this jungle. And there are terrible men in that shack who are trapping birds and animals. They even have a baby orang-utan. It's going to die unless someone helps it soon. Please, you've got to help me."

"Sounds like it," Leonardo-guy replied. "Let's see what we can do." He smiled, showing very white, very small teeth. Then he took Megan's arm and turned her back in the direction of the shack.

"No! No!" Megan shook her head. "We can't go back there."

"I'm afraid we have to," Leonardo-guy replied.

"Hey, Buddy! Sam! We've got company," he called,

and took hold of her elbow.

It was now or never. Grab your chance, the karate instructor had said. Thank you, Mom, for insisting on karate self-defense lessons. Megan allowed him to pull her back and then fell against him, stomped hard on his instep, and brought her elbow back and up against his chin. Leonardo-guy yelped in shock and let go of her arm.

Megan ran.

Roaring in anger, the man came after her.

Heart pounding, Megan picked up speed, slipping and sliding on the trail. She could hear the poacher's rasping breathing right behind her. As she forced her legs faster, a hand like steel gripped her arm and the furious poacher whipped her around and slapped her face, hard. Warm blood poured from her nose. She tried to bring up her knee and slam his groin, but he grabbed her leg and shoved her backward. For a moment she felt a thrill of satisfaction when she saw he had blood running from his mouth. Then, eyes narrowed in fury, he pulled her to her feet, bent her wrist down enough so she knew it would break if she struggled, and jerked her toward the shack.

CHAPTER 8

Sydney twisted on her lumpy bracken bed, bumped her head on a rock, and woke up. She could smell the heat as the morning sun broiled the muddy cave and overhanging branches. She wished she could smell bacon instead.

She looked around the dimly lit cave. Adam and Luke looked sweet asleep. Luke's red-brown, tangled hair covered his eyes. He had two bright-pink mosquito bites on his cheeks. Adam lay on his stomach. His white T-shirt was streaked with mud and sweat. She wished she could save them all. Take them home. Take them to Disneyland and buy pizzas for everyone. Reaching over, she shook Luke's arm. "Where's Megs?"

Luke sat up and rubbed his eyes. "I don't know. Is it

morning?"

"Looks like it." Sydney wriggled out through the cave opening and stared around. The air smelled fresh and the warmth of the sun felt good. Thank heavens the night was over. Things always felt much better and less scary in the morning. She opened one of the poachers' cans of ravioli and scooped some out with her fingers, then passed the can to Adam and Luke.

"Wish I could light a fire," Adam said. "My grandfather always said it took a real man to do that."

"Tastes good cold," Luke said. "Can I have some more?"

"Leave some for Megs. Let's go wash in the bayou." Sydney jumped to her feet. "Come on, Adam, you smell like a porcupine."

"You don't know what a porcupine smells like."

"I do—it smells like you." Sydney scrambled down the bank to the water. She had Adam all to herself. The morning had improved considerably. She sneaked a look at him as he slid down the bank. He was cute. And he was nice, too.

The creek shone like a copper mirror. A large blue heron flapped its wings and took off into the sky. Sydney scratched a mosquito bite on her arm and looked dreamily at two pink flamingos that stood on one leg each at the edge of the water. Magical. Sometimes the swampland was magical.

Adam grabbed her arm and pulled her back up the bank.

"What's wrong?"

"Look!" Adam pointed in front of her. A glistening

dark-brown alligator lay hidden, the top of his head peeking out of the water. One slit eye watched them. "Those gators are very fast. They'll pull you into the water with their tails and drown you. Then they'll eat you."

Sydney grimaced and nodded. "Point taken, thanks. Where's Megs, anyway?"

"I hope she didn't go back to get that orangutan," Luke said. "What are those men doing? Why are they hiding animals here?"

"They've smuggled them into the US, and they're going to sell them," Adam said. "Those are rare animals. My Uncle Joe used to work for the Customs Department in Miami. He says thousands of wildlife shipments come through Miami International every month. That airport is first in the US for live animal trafficking."

"But doesn't someone check the crates?"

"Not all of them. My uncle said the airport has only six wildlife agents. They can't open every crate. Animals like that baby orangutan are worth a fortune. Smuggling animals is a billion-dollar trade."

"But why do people buy them?" Luke said.

"Some people like unusual pets. They want a rare parrot or a big, bird-eating spider. My uncle says the poachers get false papers. They say the orangutan is an orphan or comes from another zoo and was born in captivity—sometimes people just don't care. They buy illegal stuff because they want to dress in leathers and exotic furs."

"That's so sick," Luke said. "Did you see the little monkeys with the white bits of fur at their ears? Did you see their tiny hands pulling the bars?"

"I bet that's where Megan's gone," Sydney said. "She's going to try to get the orangutan, and she's going to get us into a worse mess, as usual."

"Luke and I'll go down there and look for her," Adam said. "You can wait in the cave if you like."

Sydney watched the two boys head off, pushing their way through the bushes and trees along the trail, and then she sighed and walked down to the creek. She inspected the murky water for alligators and then quickly splashed her face and tried to untangle her long hair.

The bayou flowed fast after the storm. A fish jumped out in front of her, and she started back. She wished she could catch one. Adam would be impressed if she caught a fish for breakfast. She'd noted the way alligators lay there so still, motionlessly waiting for their prey. Maybe, if she just hovered near the fish, she could grab one. Little red crabs darted out of sight. A brown pelican flew by. All the fish had disappeared, seeming to know she was there.

She felt nervous all alone and started up the bank to the cave. It was just typical of Megan to go wandering off without telling anyone. She jumped to attention as she heard the noise of someone crashing through the bushes. Adam and Luke came running up, faces tense. Wide-eyed with fear, Luke looked about to cry.

"What's happening? Where's Megs?"

"She's been caught by the poachers." Adam's voice sounded raspy. "She's in the shack. We could hear her shouting."

"We've got to get her out of there!"

"There are at least three men," Luke said. "We could hear them."

"We'll try to get her when it's dark," Adam said. "The men will guess Megan's not alone. They'll come looking for us. It's easy to kill in the Glades. No one knows we're here. You keep watch while Luke and I try to repair the boat. Whistle if you hear or see anyone coming. Do an owl's call, like this." He pursed his lips together and gave a low series of whistles. "And hide all our stuff so no one can see where we are."

Sick with anxiety, Sydney began pulling down the tarpaulin. She pushed everything into the cave and draped vines and leaves over the front of the shelter. Every few minutes, she stared in the direction of the shack, listening, her ears pricking with effort for any unusual noises. What was happening to Megs? How dangerous were the men? Would they really kill?

CHAPTER 9

Adam and Luke stomped through the muddy, ankle-deep water to where parts of the boat and propeller fan showed through the black, lightning-seared branches of the burned mahogany tree..

"Okay," Adam said. "Let's see what's left." He grabbed a branch and began pulling and tugging at it, trying to free the boat. Luke grabbed the other end, pulling in unison. Soon they were streaming with sweat and covered with mud and charcoal.

Adam hauled at the charred branches, breathing heavily. "Push it back and forth; I think it's coming loose." They'd been working for hours, and he felt exhausted. And they still had to work out a way of saving Megan. He couldn't even begin to think how they would do that.

Together, they shoved the boat, bracing their feet in the sucking mud. It moved. Adam raised a fist in triumph. "It's floating! Push it farther into the channel. I can't see the engine or the propeller." He broke off a six-foot branch, poked around in the deep water at the back of the boat, and tried to locate the engine, but the mud rose and bubbled like a pot of voodoo soup.

"Here's an oar!" Luke pulled an oar out of the mud. "I'll look for the other one." Taking a deep breath, he put his face into the muddy water.

"Try to find the engine," Adam said. "We may be able to fix it. It's going to be difficult to get away without it."

Luke came up, wiping his eyes. "Can't see a thing."

Adam felt sick with fear and responsibility. He should never have brought these Californian kids into the Glades. He should have refused. He'd wanted to impress the girls; they were so cute. He'd been helping out at the dock when they'd turned up at the store. Luke and Megan had spotted two big alligators from the boardwalk, and they were buzzing with excitement. He'd heard them begging their parents to take them on an airboat ride, and he'd felt like nodding in agreement—how could anyone not want to explore the twisting canals leading into the swamplands? Mostly, he avoided the tourists, but these three had been so friendly, so nice. And now they were all in this terrible mess.

What if those poachers killed Megan? He'd be responsible. Just like when his dad died. Like a horror movie whirring in reverse, his mind took him back to that terrible night: the smoke choking him as he woke, coughing, and the hiss and crackle of the fire and the heat. His bedroom was on the ground floor, and he'd raced outside, seeing the flames running like lightning across the living room floor. The firemen had arrived fast and asked if anyone was in there. He'd said no. His mom was still at work—she was on the night shift at the hospital—and his dad was at the pub.

Then he'd heard his dog barking, and he pushed past the firemen and into the flames. Why didn't he think that maybe his dad had come home? And that maybe he was crashed out, drunk, in bed? All he'd thought about was saving Turbo.

Then the firemen had started shouting that they'd found someone in there, and he realized it was his dad. But it was too late. He knew his mom blamed him. He blamed himself. And now these kids' parents would blame him, too. It was his fault.

He poked around in the mud, trying to find the other oar. It was a long way back to the Florida Bay campground. How was he going to get them all there in an airboat without an engine or even oars? He turned to Luke. "You keep on looking for those oars. Call Sydney to help you. I'm going back to the shack."

"But how will you get Megs?"

"I'll think of something."

The air exploded with sound. A bullet sizzled across the water and smashed into Adam's calf. Instinctively, he leaped over the side of the airboat and covered his head with his arms. "Get down, Luke. Get down!"

A series of shots rang out. Luke screamed a horrible,

blood-chilling scream. Adam lifted his head in time to see Luke, bent over and clutching his shoulder, stagger and fall into the water.

Adam dove into the creek. He felt furiously around the soupy water, trying to find his friend. A second later, another gunshot burst the air. Adam came up for air and looked around frantically before taking a deep breath and diving down again. Where was Luke? He pulled his way through reeds and groped around in the mud. Nothing.

He looked up quickly to where he'd last seen Sydney. Where was she? Shouts came from the surrounding mangroves. Two men were splashing their way through the mangroves toward the boat. He had to get out of there. He shoved at the boat and hung on to the side as the current caught and it started moving slowly down the river. His leg throbbed, and he reached down to check his calf and then stared in dismay at his blood-covered hand. Great. He was bleeding to death in the Glades. Come along, alligators, dinner's ready!

Hoisting himself up, he tumbled into the boat. Blood streamed down his leg. Trembling, he grabbed a tangled mass of vines, ripped them loose, and pressed them into the wound. The blood still seeped through. "Go! Go!" he urged the boat. It was moving faster now, but the men were still coming, pushing through the mangroves and mud. Another gunshot shattered the night. Then he heard whooping shouts. "Come out. Come out, wherever you are!"

A bullet ricocheted across the water, spinning off the side of the boat. I'm being hunted like one of those animals, he thought. The boat hit a bend full of long saw grass and vines, floundered, and then stopped. Oh God, they're going to get me. Please, God, help me get out of here. He jumped back into the water and pushed, trying to force the boat through the grass. Something moved on his right. He whipped around, peering into the black grass. A dark, torpedo-like shape slithered through the grass and two red eyes stared back at him. He was right in an alligator's pantry.

He heard a splash as the alligator slid into the water. Headfirst, he dived back into the relative safety of the boat. The thing could smell his blood. It was coming for him! And it was big, too. Big enough to flip the boat. Tearing off another handful of reeds and grass, he frantically tied them around his bleeding wound. How could he hide the smell of blood?

Cupping his hand to hold the urine, he peed carefully down his leg, soaking the wound. Perhaps the urine would cover the smell of blood, but would it also attract the alligator? He could hear the men catcalling, and his head spun with confusion. Why did they sound as if they were at a party and having some great time? Had they found Sydney and Luke?

Huddled on the small boat, he felt dizzy with fear and terribly alone.

CHAPTER 10

The sound of gunshots and shouting filled the air. Fighting panic, Sydney looked around wildly. All she could see was jungle. What was happening? She dived into the shelter and sat there, shivering. There wasn't a thought in her head of any use to her. Were the poachers trying to kill Luke and Adam? She had to help. But what could she do?

For what seemed like hours, she huddled there. In the distance, she could hear the men shouting and laughing. Bile rose in her throat. Any minute, she was going to vomit with fear. The sun was setting. Outside the shelter, she could see glimpses of pink and red clouds streaked across the sky. There was no sound or sign of Adam and Luke. She knew she couldn't just sit here in safety when everyone else was in danger, although she wished she could. If the men were chasing the two boys, they must have left Megs alone. She hoped so. Maybe she could save her sister. Megs would know what to do next.

She crawled out of the shelter and began making her way through the undergrowth along the long trail to the shack. The Glades shrieked around her. She felt like the victim in a horror movie, the babysitter type who goes into the wild woods when everyone knows she should just stay at home.

The trail seemed much longer than she remembered. Every corner posed a potential threat. Anything could be lurking or hunting. Night was when these creatures ate. And darkness was coming fast. Darkness in the Glades would be really, really dark. For the millionth time, she wished she'd worn jeans. Her skin gleamed so white here, in the dark jungle. The better to see you with, my dear, she thought. She'd always loved reading *Little Red Riding Hood*. Now the thought of the big, bad, hungry wolf totally spooked her. She scooped up mud and covered her legs, arms, and face. The mud would hide her skin. Maybe it would hide her human smell, too. She kept her eyes on the trail, not daring to look to either side. She was sure, if she looked hard, she'd see red eyes gleaming from the dark behind the trees.

At last the shack loomed in front of her. She stopped and listened. Everything was silent. Her heart thumped. The bathroom window was still partly open. She could climb in there. Sure she could. But, omigod, she didn't want to.

She was so scared. What if she left right now? Ran all the way back to the shelter and hid there, hoping to be rescued? Surely, sooner or later, her mom and dad would come. But what if they came too late? What if Megs or Adam or Luke was badly hurt and needed help right now, and she, Sydney, was too wimpy to save them? What if Megs was inside here, a prisoner, or hurt? What if one of the poachers or one of the animals had gotten to Megs? Do it! she told herself. Just do it!

She could shout for Megs, but what if the men were close by? They'd hear her. She had no option; she just had to go inside. She forced herself to climb through the window and dropped down to the bathroom floor. Catching a glimpse of herself in the bathroom window, she almost shrieked. With her eyes outlined in dark mud, she looked fierce. Like some sort of female Amazonian warrior, eyes bright and gleaming. For a moment, she felt a thrill of something almost like power. She could do this. Sydney, the warrior. She walked fast and silent toward the awful-smelling living room. Inside, it was almost dark and filled with shadows. Animals in the cages squeaked and chattered. The little orangutan ran to the bars of his cage and shook them. Sydney looked at him with sympathy but turned away. She had to find Megs before the men returned.

First she ran to the kitchen. There was no sign of Megan anywhere. Adjacent to the kitchen door, she saw concrete stairs leading down. Up here was bad enough. The thought of going down into the dark below the stairs made her almost faint with fear. "Megs!" she called as loudly as she dared. No reply. She tried to ignore the awful, nagging thought that maybe Megs was so silent because Megs was dead.

She felt along the wall for a light switch. There wasn't one. Did they have electricity out here? Maybe not. She'd seen an oil lamp. Maybe there'd be matches or a lighter. She looked around the kitchen and sighed with relief when she saw a flashlight on a shelf. The circle of light on the stairwell wall showed dark blood-colored stains dotting the stairs. No way did she want to go down into the cellar below. It was dark down there—dungeon dark.

She took a deep breath. She had to go down. But what if the poachers returned while she was in the cellar with no escape and nowhere to run?

"Megs," she whispered. Still louder, "Megan?" No reply. Listening for the sounds of anyone returning, her heart pounding from her stomach to her chest, she went down the stairs.

The cellar in front of her looked like a slaughterhouse. Animal bones and skins littered the floor, and shelves of guns glinted as she moved the light around. So the men were arms dealers, too. Great. They'd have plenty of guns. All the better to kill us with.

She picked up a sinister-looking hunting rifle and held it gingerly. She had no idea if it was loaded or not, or if the safety catch was on. Not happy to lug it around, she replaced it. She'd find Megs first. Megs might know how to load the thing.

Another door waited. She took a deep breath and opened it, feeling as if she were suffocating. The air smelled even worse down here, like blood and dust. As her eyes adjusted to the gloom, she made out a small shape curled on the floor.

"Megan! Megs!" she cried. There was total silence. Maybe it wasn't Megs. Maybe it was another dead animal. Or maybe it was a live, injured animal about to spring at her. The figure moved. Sydney jumped back and steadied the flashlight, then saw with relief that it was Megs, her legs and arms tied together, with tape over her mouth.

"Megs!"

Megan made an awful gurgling sound. Sydney grabbed her face and ripped the tape off slowly, trying not to hurt her whimpering sister. Fumbling in the dark, she pulled out a sock, or something woolen, crammed in Megan's mouth.

Megan gasped in relief and licked her lips in an effort to talk. "Oh, Sydney! Get me loose. We have to get out of here." She thrust her hands and feet in Sydney's direction, showing the tightly knotted ropes.

"I'll need a knife," Sydney said. "Right, I'll find one. Just wait, Megs. I'll save you. Everything will be fine. I can do it. Wait!"

She stumbled up the stairs and into the kitchen, quickly looking around to see if anyone had returned. The only sound was water dripping into the blood in the sink. She grabbed a large, evil-looking knife and made her way back downstairs. Careful not to cut Megan, she sawed through the rope, and Megan rose shakily to her feet.

Her hand tight on her sister's arm, Sydney pulled her in the direction of the stairs. "Hurry! Hurry! Those guys are shooting at Luke and Adam. This is so bad, Megs. We've got to help."

"Wait. I can't leave without Baby Furball," Megan said. "I can't leave him here."

"No!" Sydney wailed. "We have to get away from here!"

"Just help me. Quick!" Megan ran around the cages, opening them one after another. The animals inside cowered away from her, frightened. Sydney choked back sobs of frustration. Then, as Megan clearly wasn't going to leave until the animals had been freed, she started to rush around, too, opening cages.

After lifting the little orangutan into her arms and balancing him on her hip, Megan pulled open the front door. It opened one inch and jammed, caught by the chain. "How are we going to get the animals out? There's a chain on the door."

"I can't believe this, Megs! I just can't believe it!" Wide-eyed, Sydney looked around the room. Most of the cages were open. Within moments, the animals could be free of the cages but stuck in the room. They were wild and frightened. Not a good combination. She shivered.

A big golden gibbon had already crept out and was sitting on the top of his cage. He looked right in Sydney's direction and bared his long, pointed teeth. "One minute, dude," she said, trying to sound as calm as she could.

"How can we get them out of here?" Megan's jagged bangs stood up from her head; her eyes looked wild. Sydney stared at her. Was she nuts? Forget the animals; they'd make it some way or another. She and Megs needed to get out of there themselves before they got stung, bitten, or mauled. "They'll work it out. Let's just get out of here, ourselves. Bring the orangutan with you."

She pushed open the large living room window. Cool night air wafted into the room. With a flap of wings, two large scarlet macaws flew out into the night, followed by twittering red-and-green parrots, and a group of giant fruit bats.

The golden gibbons stood for a moment, unsure of what was happening. Then they grunted at each other, raised their arms into the air in a gesture of freedom, and scurried past the two girls, making for the open window.

"Okay." Sydney smiled encouragingly at the worried-looking Megan. "I'll climb out the window first, and you can hand him to me. The rest of the animals are watching. Hopefully, they'll work it out, too."

"We have to save all the animals, Sydney. Those turtles and tortoises will never get out the window."

Sydney groaned and dashed back to the turtles' cage. She picked up four small turtles and leaned out the window, reaching down as far as she could with each one so they softly plunked the short distance to the ground. Then she did the same thing for the tortoises. After opening the snakes' cages, she dashed back to the window, ready to climb out. Megan seemed frozen to the spot, but Sydney knew what she wanted to do. She wanted to leave—like yesterday, already. "So now can we go? I'm not picking up the snakes. I'm sure they'll manage."

Lifting its head, a large green python slid out of its cage and slithered across the floor.

"See! They've got the picture!" Sydney cried. Together, she, Megan, and the small orangutan scrambled out over the windowsill. They ran for the shelter of the surrounding bushes and stood, looking back.

The shack looked like Noah's Ark in reverse as birds flew out into the night and animals scampered off into the rainforest. For a magic moment, two timid Key deer peeked over the sill before springing out into the beckoning moonlight.

"We did it!" Sydney patted the little orangutan. "Let's go!"

They started running down the trail. A gunshot echoed in the distance.

"Those men are shooting at Luke and Adam," Sydney cried. "We've got to do something."

Megan stopped and thought for a moment. Then her eyes sparkled. "Let's burn down the shack. They'll see the fire and smoke. The animals are worth a lot of money to them, and they'll think they're all burning up. I bet they race back here and leave the boys. It's old, dry wood. It'll be easy to burn—let's do it!"

They shooed the last of the parrots into the forest and pushed two large geckos away from the door. Sydney looked nervously for the snakes, but they seemed to have slithered away. She climbed back through the large window and ran to the kitchen cupboard, looking for matches.

"Look for paper," Megan called. "We'll stack it under those wooden chairs."

"We don't want to start a forest fire."

"The grass is wet; there's been a lot of rain. Besides, the house is surrounded by dirt, so it shouldn't spread. Are you sure all the animals are out of there?"

"Yes, positive."

Together, they made a pyramid of a wooden chair, crumbled newspapers, and dry branches. "Okay, take Baby Furball outside, and I'll light this," Megan said. "Wait, I think I saw some drums of helicopter fuel outside."

She grabbed two plastic buckets from the kitchen and ran out to the fuel drums, tipping them over and filling both buckets with fuel. She splashed the fuel over the pyramid and around the shack.

Sydney crouched outside with Baby Furball, who watched their activities with wide eyes. Megan stood in the doorway, lit a match, threw it into the room, and ran. For a few minutes, nothing happened. Then there was a whooshing noise, and flames and smoke rose from the doorway. Megan held out her arms for Baby Furball and, together, she and Sydney watched, stunned, at the success of their arson. A spiral of smoke and flames rose into the air. The fire spread fast. Flames crackled. Searing heat hit their faces, and they ran back into the jungle. From behind them, ammunition in the house exploded in loud, earsplitting bangs.

"Sounds like we started a war!" Megan said. "This is better than I thought it would be. Even Mom would be impressed! Hey, the whole Marine Corps would be impressed!" They held on to each other and began to laugh hysterically. The smell of burning timber filled the air.

"What if the men don't see the flames?" Sydney said.

"Of course they'll see them. They'll come back to see what's happening, and they'll try to put the fire out and salvage the animals."

"Megan!" Sydney grabbed her twin's arm. "There were guns in there. Should we have taken the guns?"

Megan stared at her and then back at the burning shack. "Too late now."

Sydney looked crestfallen. "I'm sorry. I'm an idiot."

"You did really good getting me out." Megan hugged her and turned in the direction of the river. From far away, they heard shouting, followed by two more gunshots. "Here they come! Let's get out of here!"

CHAPTER II

Still buzzing with adrenalin, Megan ran down the dark jungle trail. The baby orangutan clung to her neck, and she stumbled over roots as she tried to move as fast and silently as possible. She remembered reading that, when in the wild, whatever you do, don't run, because in the wild only the food runs. She hoped that wasn't true in the Everglades, too. She hoped the sound of their running feet wouldn't attract some big, hungry predator. Like a Florida panther.

In front of her, she could hear Sydney's pounding footsteps, and she adjusted her steps to the same pace. A sudden cool breeze whipped her cheeks, drying the sweat on her skin. Running through the forest together was nice in a way. She remembered reading that the Native

American runners had always run in pairs—running hundreds of miles to take messages or bring important news to other villages.

Sydney turned back and panted, "Come on. Faster!"

"Go ahead," Megan panted. "I'll meet you at the cave. Run as fast as you can and look for the guys." She put her cheek down to the orangutan's little furry head. "Don't worry, Baby," she whispered. "It's you and me, together. I'll never leave you."

Sydney hesitated, then nodded, and headed on along the trail.

Megan stumbled after her. She was having a hard time seeing where the trail was and where to put her feet. Baby Furball blocked her view of the ground, and he seemed to be growing heavier by the minute. She kept up her head and tried to relax her shoulder muscles and still hold him, but it was difficult. She was running through a dark tunnel of trees. Vegetation blocked whatever breeze there was. Now sweat streamed down her forehead and into her eyes. Her breath came in steamy huffs into the humid night air. Any minute now she'd get a stitch in her side.

This part of the trail had an ominous, horrible smell—a smell she remembered too well. She must be near the slough hole Luke fell into. She slowed down to take a deep, slow breath. Suddenly, the orangutan reared back against her and gave a high-pitched bark. "What? What's wrong?"

Megan stopped. Something was out there. What? Black shadows flickered between the trees. Was that a glimmer of moonlight or a glint of eyes? A panther? A black bear?

Baby Furball barked again, a series of high barks. Megan's heart raced. Something in the pitch-blackness behind the bushes let out a low growl. Baby Furball screeched and pushed his way out of Megan's arms, leaping for the nearest tree. Panic-stricken, trying to run and to grab the orangutan at the same time, Megan lunged forward. There was a big empty space where the ground should have been.

Screaming, she crashed down into the slough hole.

CHAPTER 12

Arriving at the shelter, Sydney groaned in relief and crawled inside. This place was beginning to feel like home. The first thing she did was to grab the can of DEET and soak herself in it. The plastic raincoat tied around her waist had fallen off somewhere along the trail, and the mosquitoes here were much quicker than the ones back in California. Back home, if you kept moving, you were usually okay. But not here. No. Everything was ravenous in the Everglades, including herself.

She felt exhilarated from the long run. She decided that when she got back home she'd be a lot more active—take up karate like Megs, or something—so the next time she needed to escape from hungry predators and vicious poachers, etcetera, her body would be at its best: fast, tough, ready for action.

She found another raincoat to wrap around her legs and waited with increasing anxiety. Where was Megs? Strange noises came from the darkness. Things she couldn't see but could imagine surrounded her. Where on Earth were Adam and Luke? She didn't dare call out for them, and hoped they were somewhere safe, hiding from the poachers. But what if they were lying somewhere, injured? Leaving the shelter was the last thing she felt like doing, but how could she stay here when the others were all in trouble? Reluctantly, she stood up and began to walk back down the trail.

The rainforest was like a maze, and it was so dark. She stumbled on a number of large, flat rocks she didn't remember seeing before. Had she taken a wrong turn? Perhaps she should just go back to the shelter. Perhaps Megs was already there. Snap! What was that? Someone was coming. Megs? Adam or Luke? A poacher? She crawled into the bushes, forcing her way into the dense vines and trying not to think about spiders and snakes. She'd wait a while, see if Megs came. She was glad she'd soaked herself in DEET, so at least the mosquitoes were leaving her alone.

Crack! Something or someone was close by, cracking through the vegetation. What if it was an alligator? What if she'd run toward the river and the alligators were coming out to eat? They hunted at night, didn't they? She was just part of the food chain here. Right at the bottom of the food chain. Sick with fear, she strained to keep still. A branch snapped. Eyes narrowed, she peeked through the leaves, trying to see into the night. What was out there? Another snap.

Then a voice said, "I know you're there. I can smell you. I can smell the DEET."

CHAPTER 13

Dizzy and nauseated, Megan opened her eyes and groaned. The darkness was total. She tried to sit up. Pain shot through her ankle. Wincing, she reached down and touched it tentatively. Oh no! She shuddered. Something bad had happened to her leg, and her foot was bent in the wrong position. Gingerly, she ran her fingers around her ankle, horrified as she felt a lump of bone sticking up in a way no bone should, pushing at her skin. Omigod, how would she ever get out of here with a broken ankle?

She forced herself to stay quiet. Panic wouldn't help her. If the poachers found her here, they would finish her off and wouldn't even need to bury her body. It would rot away right here in this slough hole. Awful thought. She had to stop thinking awful thoughts. This would not be the end of her. She had things to do. Many, many things. She had to save herself, and she had to save Baby Furball. Where was Baby Furball, anyway? Also, was that growling creature still lurking somewhere behind the trees? Here she was—dinner. A tasty, tender, young human nicely seasoned by dead monkey guts.

She began to whimper as she'd done when she was a little child, afraid of the dark in the middle of the night. She'd always been afraid of the dark. Mom had bought her a nightlight shaped like a shell and told her stories about a brave little girl who loved the dark. That was way before Mom got deployed to Iraq three times in two years and became all bad-tempered, like a dictator. But, dictator or not, she wished her mom were here right now. She could really use the help of a Marine! Omigod, anybody could use the help of a Marine. Where were the Marines when she needed them! Not to mention the help of a medic. What would Dad do to help a broken ankle? She tried to think, but she was so afraid, she couldn't think of anything. And it was just so horribly dark. She had no idea what was around her. She hated, just hated, the dark.

She'd read somewhere that fear of the dark meant fear of death. Duh! Someone was about to kill her—of course she was afraid of death and the dark. She felt her throat constricting. Breathing deeply in and out, she tried to give herself a pep talk. You go, girl, she told herself. Someone said bravery is being terrified and doing it anyway. No one is coming to save you. Save yourself.

She began to feel around in the mud. Surely she could pull her way up out of here. Slowly and painfully, she dragged herself to the side of the hole, crawling through thick mud and inches of water. She tried not to think of what she was crawling through and what was causing the awful, rotten, sickly-sweet smell.

Her fingers touched something hard and she pulled on it, thinking to find something to help her dig her way out. The object gleamed dull white. It was small and had holes in it. Black, gaping holes. Holes like eyes. Megan gave a muffled shriek. A skull! And right next to her elbow was a sheet of ribs. She was lying in a murky, stinking mess of skulls and bones. She touched her stinging leg again and pulled her dirty fingers away fast as she felt sticky, warm blood. Great. She had an open wound, and she was lying here in filth. What if she got gangrene?

She felt as if she was going mad.

CHAPTER 14

Sydney crouched, hardly daring to breathe. The poacher was right here! Her heart thumped so loud, she felt sure he'd hear it.

"You kids shouldn't be running around the swamplands like this," he said. "It's dangerous."

Yeah right, Sydney thought, so I gathered.

"Come on out. You need help. There's a monster alligator has his pad right down the bank a few yards away from here. They're territorial, you know. And you're like meat in his pantry. He'll be able to smell you."

Another branch snapped. He was so close.

"Come on out." The man spoke sweetly now, just your nice, friendly neighborhood poacher. "You're much too young to be out here alone. We can go back to my shack and have something hot to eat. Soup, or something. I bet you're hungry. Then I'll fly you out of here in my helicopter. You'll be back home before you know it. And then you can bring help for your friends. There are a few of you out here, aren't there? I'm sure your parents must be worried."

Hot tears trickled down Sydney's cheeks. Yes, she knew her parents would be worried. But this man wouldn't help her. Her head spun. Maybe he would. He sounded quite nice. Maybe he wasn't one of the poachers. Maybe he was just someone who lived here in the swamp. For a minute, she almost stood up—almost ran to him.

Then common sense took over. This man was bad. All he wanted was to get rid of her so she wouldn't mess up his animal poaching business.

"I won't hurt you," the man said. "I promise."

No. Leave me alone. Get away from me. I hope an alligator eats you, you creep.

"I can see you right there."

Could he see her? No. If he could, he'd have grabbed her. Trembling, she forced herself to stay motionless. Sweat trickled down her forehead, into her eyes, and down her cheeks.

The man was moving away, banging a stick or something at the bushes. He didn't know where she was! Sydney dared a shallow breath.

"Hey!"

There he was again!

"It's a rush being in the Glades in the dark, isn't it?"

He chuckled. "All those gators. There are thousands of them, you know. Big-toothed lizards, and some of them four hundred pounds! Ever see their eyes at night? Red. Real slit-eyed and mean. Hungry. And the way they lie there, their eyes just above the water, watching, waiting. Threw my dad's dog into the swamp once—right next to a humongous one—but the dumb dog got away. Never saw a dog swim so fast."

Sydney shivered. Silence again. Had he gone? Thank you, God! But what about the alligators? A gunshot rang in the distance. The man swore and muttered something to himself. When he spoke again, he sounded angry. "Bet that big gator is sniffing for you right now," he said. "Serve you right if it grabs you and drags you under and takes you on a nice-old death roll. That's what you kids are asking for—looking for trouble, snooping around in the swamplands."

For a moment, she almost told him she wasn't snooping around in the swamplands. He could have the swamplands. All she wanted to do was go home. She pressed her lips together and stayed quiet.

She heard bushes rustling. Was he going off to help his buddies? Didn't he know his place was burning down?

For what seemed like hours, she stayed huddled in the bushes, legs smarting with pins and needles, shoulders cramped. She was half asleep when a branch snapped again. He was back! Then she heard the owl call, the call Adam had taught her! Her heart leaped with joy. Adam! She licked her dry lips and whistled, trying to imitate the sound. No answer. She tried again and, to her relief, heard a responding whistle. It was Adam! She jumped up and ran to him, throwing her arms around his neck, pressing her face into his shoulder.

"Oh, Adam, thank heavens you're here," she whispered. "One of the poachers almost got me. He could still be around here somewhere, so be really quiet. And I found Megs. I had her with me, but she's disappeared again. I don't know what's happened to her."

Adam sank down in the leaves and grasped his injured leg.

"What happened to your leg?"

"It'll be all right. We have to get away from here. Those men are killers. They had no problem shooting at Luke and me. They're going to keep hunting us."

"Where's Luke?"

Adam looked at her and shook his head in despair. "I don't know, Sydney. I think he was shot. He fell into the creek. I looked for him all over. I thought he might have managed to drag himself out onto the bank. I couldn't find him."

Sydney stared at him in horror, feeling totally unreal. She pictured Luke lying somewhere in the mud, shot and dying. For a minute, everything in front of her eyes went gray, and she sank down into the mud beside Adam. Tears rolled down her cheeks, and she began to sob.

Adam put his arm around her shoulders and pulled her to him. "I'm so sorry."

She wiped her nose on her hand. She had to pull

herself together. Besides, Luke could be alive. He was a good swimmer. But what if he was injured? There wasn't time to cry. They had to find him. She loved her brother so much. She'd shared a bedroom with him once, when he was only a toddler. They'd grown so close, giggled at night, and read his favorite book, *Where the Wild Things Are,* again and again, safely tucked under the blankets. They'd found the wild things, now.

She jumped to her feet. "We've got to find him."

"I tried," Adam said. "He isn't there. He might have been washed down the river. That's my best hope." He rubbed his eyes. "This is all so terrible. Where's Megan?"

"We set fire to the shack," Sydney said. "We freed all of the animals, and we were running away. Megs was carrying the baby orangutan, so she was slower than me. But she should be here by now."

Adam groaned. "Stay here. I'll go back along the trail for a while and see if I can find her."

"Be careful. One of the poachers is around. And the alligators."

Sydney huddled in the dark. It seemed an age before Adam pushed through the bushes in front of her.

"Quick! The men are coming this way, I heard them on the trail," he said. "We've got to get out of here and get help. We can't fight a group of men with guns. The boat is floating okay; I can pole it along with an oar. I've hidden it in a clump of saw grass. We'll watch out for Luke. Maybe he's hiding and he'll spot us."

Adam took Sydney's hand, and they leaned against

each other, exhausted. Then they made their way down the bank, along the river, Adam leading through the mangroves and mud.

Globs of slimy mud oozed into Sydney's broken sneakers and mashed between her toes. Each step was a big effort. She tried not to think about alligators. She felt panic boil in her throat but fought it down. Surely Luke was alive. Surely Megs would suddenly appear. Her jaw hurt, and she realized she was clenching her teeth. A spiderweb brushed her face, covering it with a fine, sticky film. Grimacing as she brushed it off, she felt something fat and squishy land in her hair. She yelped. "Adam! What's in my hair?"

Adam brushed her head with his hand. "Ssh. It's just a leaf, relax. We don't want those men to hear us. Wait for me here; I'll find the boat."

Sydney cringed in the mangroves as he waded into the dark, murky water. Then he whistled and she waded after him, relieved to see the familiar shape of the airboat. The water felt warm. Reeds brushed against her legs. Every touch felt like an alligator's skin.

"Get in," he said. "The engine's gone. It's sort of like a raft, now. I'll push us. Let's move!"

Pushing the one oar into the mucky creek, he poled them through the saw grass and into the open canal.

CHAPTER 15

Adam poled hard, planting the oar against the soft bottom again and again and leaning against it as he shoved the boat forward. Black mangrove roots blocked the creek at several spots. It was very dark and quiet; the only sounds were the lapping of the water and the hooting of animals. As he leaned his weight on the pole, he kept a close watch on the banks and the surrounding water, hoping he would spot Luke or Megan.

"Do you know which way to go?" Sydney asked.

"I hope I do. More or less, anyway," he replied, talking softly. "We were in all those twisting channels as we came through, and it's going to take much longer getting back this way without a motor. We have to find the bay and then try to get to the campground. I think we'll have to make our way the long way around, going right around the edges of the bay and keeping to the shallows where I can pole us along. I've never done that. I guess it's possible, though it's a long way."

"I wish we were back at the campground," Sydney groaned.

"We will be. Eventually." Adam pushed hard at the oar. "It's the maze of mangrove islands and side canals that are messing me up. The tide seems to be going out. If we go with the drift, it should take us in the direction of the bay."

Little waves splashed the boat, and Sydney shivered and huddled up on the seat. Water sloshed around her feet. The channel narrowed, and the current picked up, pulling them through a black canopy of moss-laden trees. Sydney could picture eyes watching them from the shadows. She shuddered.

Adam pointed to a group of bright stars. "Check out the Pleiades over there. Indians have lots of stories about them. Some say they were seven girls who were attacked by a bear and escaped to the sky. They are always said to be friends who help each other and stay together. Like us."

"That's nice." Sydney gave a tentative smile.

"Try to take a nap; you'll feel better."

Sydney nodded. She was so tired.

She seemed to have closed her eyes for only a moment. When she opened them the sky had grown lighter. Dawn was coming. She was so stiff! And she absolutely had to go to the toilet.

Adam turned and smiled at her, putting down the oar.

He stretched and groaned. "That's some exercise."

"Can we go into shore soon?"

"Yeah, we'll have to get out of sight. I think those guys had a helicopter, and it's getting light enough for them to fly over and spot us."

The boat rocked as they entered into a larger river, and the water roiled and bubbled. A school of silvery mullet leaped out of the water, and Adam made a wild swipe at them. The boat rocked.

"Don't!" Sydney gasped. "You'll tip us out. Look at what's waiting on the bank over there."

A huge mother alligator lay in the mud, her slit eyes half open and watching. A baby alligator lay on her back, napping. Probably the safest place to lie, Sydney thought. Six more toy-like alligators swam lazily around. The boat swung close to them and Sydney shrank back. Adam rubbed his stiff shoulders. Suddenly, he tensed. "Can you hear something?"

"Like what?"

"A roar, a noise like a helicopter."

Sydney caught her breath. Was someone coming to help them? Maybe her parents were coming? Or were the poachers hunting them? They'd be sitting targets in the boat.

"We've got to get out of sight." Adam jumped into the water and pushed the boat as fast and as hard as he could into a tunnel of mangrove trees. They were just in time. The helicopter appeared, flying low and slow. Hunting.

"Duck down," Adam said.

Sydney closed her eyes and prayed fervently, "Don't let them see us. Please, please, God, don't let them see us."

There was a splash to the side. The alligator, its tail twitching, slithered toward them, staring right at Sydney. Mesmerized, Sydney stared back and yelped, "Adam!"

"Stay still!" Adam, still in the water and hanging on to the side of the boat, was peering at the helicopter.

"Quick! Get in," she stammered. "Get back in the boat, Adam."

With a sudden burst of speed, the alligator lunged, a fury of green scales and a flash of teeth. Adam leaped back into the boat and Sydney clutched him as it tipped. The alligator slid submarine-style through the dark shallows and surfaced with a small, struggling turtle in its jaws. Sydney and Adam looked at each other, speechless.

"Okay," Adam said. "Let's try that one more time."

"You'll get better at it," Sydney smiled, still breathing fast. "You were fast but clumsy."

"Oh, clumsy!"

"Anyway, you sort of smell better now. The water must have helped. Now you smell like something that died yesterday instead of last month."

"Yeah, thanks." Adam grinned. Together they scanned the sky. The helicopter had disappeared. "We'd better stay hidden here until dark. It looks like this creek widens out into the bay. We'll try to cross it tonight."

The tunnel of trees formed a canopy of green over their heads. The boat rocked gently, lapped by the rippling water. Adam pulled off his wet T-shirt and moved closer to Sydney so he could hang it over the wooden seat to dry. Sydney watched him and then quickly looked away. Megs was right—Adam was totally cute!

"We could try to catch some fish," she said. She pulled an oyster off the mangrove roots and handed it to Adam.

He smiled. "You have it."

She shook her head. "I'm still not starving enough for the live oysters."

Adam grinned. "Hey, I forgot. I have a real treat for you!" He lifted the cracked lid of the seat and triumphantly held up the remains of a packet. "Oreos! Two! One each."

"Ooh!" Sydney had never been so glad to see Oreo cookies.

Adam laughed. "I was saving them for a treat, but then we found the food in the shack. Lucky, yeah?"

"Mmm!" Sydney dropped the oyster back into the water. Licking her lips, she took a tiny bite. "Mmm!" she said. "Heaven!"

Adam smiled. He has such a nice mouth, she thought. I like the way it sort of turns up at the corners.

"Thank you," she said. "Totally yummy." Spontaneously, she leaned toward him and kissed his cheek, her lips landing just at the corner of his mouth. His skin felt warm, and he tasted like the chocolate cookie.

He turned his face toward her, and she looked into his dark eyes. Was he going to kiss her? She hoped so. She looked again at his lips.

Adam leaned forward and, looking into her eyes, kissed her softly. Her heart beat faster. She closed her eyes and began to kiss him back. Now her heart was racing. Suddenly, her world changed and she forgot the swamp around her. Her world was just Adam. She snuggled closer. He felt so warm and strong. She wrapped her arms around him and clung to him.

The boat rocked.

Adam pulled back. With one arm still holding her, he whirled around, staring at the water. "What was that?"

There was a sudden series of small taps. Peering down into the water, she saw a school of silver fish darting around the boat, fighting over the oyster and knocking the sides of the boat.

Adam grabbed his shirt and slid his arms into it, then held the garment under the water. He waited until the fish swam into the makeshift net and then quickly lifted it up. He gave a muffled whoop of triumph as three fish landed on Sydney's knees. She scrambled out of the way and looked in the opposite direction. Having been fishing before, she knew what was coming next, and she didn't want to watch Adam cut the fishes' throats. When she looked back, he was hacking the fish into strips with a penknife that didn't look very sharp.

"We'll hang them on twigs to dry," he said. "They won't taste bad like that."

Sydney grimaced at the blood. "I'm not that starving."

"You may be soon," Adam said.

Sydney nodded, thinking that, by the time the fish dried into anything she just might eat, she'd be dead of starvation. Besides, she really would have preferred more of the kissing.

Adam pointed as a large bird soared across the sky.

Sydney peered up. "What is it?"

"A bald eagle," Adam smiled. "We're lucky to see one—they're pretty rare."

"You love it here, don't you?"

Adam nodded. "It's the best. I want a job like my uncle. It'd be great to be a park ranger and spend your day taking people out into the Glades and showing them around."

Sydney nodded. "I'd like to work outside, too. I don't know what. It's hard to decide, isn't it?"

"Park ranger for me," Adam said. "I'll apply for my uncle's job when he retires. He says he's going to retire any day. Complains he doesn't make enough money, but money isn't everything."

"So you don't miss Miami?"

"Nope."

"How old were you when you left?"

"Twelve." Adam turned away and looked out at the bay.

Sydney swallowed hard. She sneaked another quick look at Adam. So he was only around twelve years old when his dad had died in the fire. Why did he feel so responsible? She thought she should say something but decided not to. Later, when she knew him better, she'd tell him that. Tell him it wasn't his fault. He didn't need to carry around that load of guilt.

Overhead, dark clouds spread across the sky. Suddenly, rain pelted down. With her face turned up and her hands cupped, Sydney gulped at the raindrops. Adam made a dive for the equipment under the bench and pulled out a piece of plastic. As he struggled to rig some sort of water-catching device, the rain stopped. They shared the trickle of raindrops on the plastic.

"I should have thought of getting ready for rain sooner," Adam said.

"I should have, too." Sydney shrugged, quickly changing the subject. "What would you eat right now if you could have anything you want?"

"Fries," he replied. "A burger, hot fries, and a cold Coke."

"Sounds great."

"What about you?"

"Double-chocolate ice cream with chocolate chunks."

They smiled at each other, and Sydney moved her feet so their toes were almost touching. A few days ago, in what seemed like another life, she'd painted her toenails silver-blue, and now they shined strangely in the muddy mess. Adam's feet looked much more utilitarian; they were large and callused, practical-looking feet.

"We'll get back to the campground faster if we can cut across the bay instead of going around in the shallows," Adam said. "But the water's deeper, and we both may have to pole. I'll find a few thick branches. Are you a good swimmer?"

"Yes," Sydney said. Actually, she didn't think she was a very good swimmer at all, but she didn't want to say so. She wanted to find help as quickly as possible. She didn't want to be the reason they took longer, plodding around the edge of the bay while goodness knows what was happening to Luke and Megs.

She studied their feet again. If she had to choose feet for crossing an alligator-ridden bay, she would choose Adam's. She decided that when and if she ever reached home, she would lift weights every day.

"Eat an oyster!" Adam urged her, scooping gray flesh out of the shiny oyster shell. "We have to keep up our strength. What if we can't find the campground?"

"I thought you said you knew where it was." Sydney heard the whining tone in her voice and stopped. Adam was doing the best he could. It wasn't fair to complain. She reached out to take the oyster and swallowed it as quickly as she could. It tasted salty and slimy. She licked her lips. She was so thirsty and hungry.

It seemed everything in the wild spent most of its time looking for food. Great blue heron stood perfectly still along the shore waiting for fish. Sydney noticed one swaying, imitating the movement of the water to lure its prey closer. Patience. These animals of the Everglades had to be very patient. It wasn't possible to do anything easily here. Eat or be eaten. Nature was hard and uncompromising. The heron plunged its head into the water and came up with a fish impaled on the end of its sharp beak. Lunch. Someone was actually having lunch.

"It's too bad we have to wait till dark," Adam said. "Florida Bay is sort of scary in the dark."

Sydney shivered. She thought that was a huge understatement. She moved toward Adam, and he wrapped an arm around her shoulders and pulled her closer. She felt his lips kissing her hair, and she lifted up her face. There was a way of making the scary and dark things go away for a while, and she'd just discovered it.

CHAPTER 16

The moon slowly rose. Megan watched as slivers of moonlight seeped into the hole, lighting up the various gruesome sights, like a spotlight in Disneyland's Tower of Terror. She'd crawled as far as she could from the skulls and bones, and she glanced over in their direction. She didn't actually want to see them, yet she felt a horrible fascination to see what was there. They were very small bones. As she looked closer, she realized she was looking at the bones of a little hand. Little hands just like Baby Furball's. Monkey bones. Nauseous, she wondered again where the baby orangutan had gone. She doubted he'd be able to fend for himself in the wild. Had she freed him only to have him eaten by something big and hungry?

She looked up at the dripping branches way above

her. She was so thirsty, and her mouth was dry, her lips chapped. To drink any of the water in the hole would be suicidal, but maybe the water dripping down would be safe. She held up her hands to catch the drops but changed her mind. Her hands were filthy. She let the drops slide onto the top of her arm and cautiously licked the areas with the least grime and mud.

Reluctantly, she looked at her foot and shuddered. Bent as it was, it looked to be almost at a right angle to her leg. She couldn't just leave it like that. She'd have to straighten it. She took a deep breath and held her leg in both hands. Her ankle was swollen, blue, and very painful. Teeth clenched, she pushed her foot straight with one fierce movement. The bones made a horrible, soft grinding sound. Groaning in pain, she looked down fearfully. At least she could no longer see the jutting bone. It didn't feel any better, however, and there was a bloody, open cut on her calf. She squeezed it to try to clean it. Luckily, her jeans covered it. Flies swarmed, smelling the blood.

She curled back into a little ball of misery, closed her eyes, and tried to sleep. Surely Sydney would be able to find her. She hadn't gone so far off of the usual trail. In fact, she was pretty sure this was the hole Luke fell into. Why hadn't they found her by now? She dreamed she was drowning, slipping deeper and deeper into a dark ocean. She shouted and called to Sydney, who just sat on the beach, licking an ice cream cone and ignoring her.

She woke to a chorus of screeching birds. Thankful it was nearly dawn, Megan peered out into the rainforest.

Every fat, hanging vine looked like a fat, hanging snake. She gasped. A pair of eyes glowed from the clump of roots just above the hole. Then another pair.

The eyes moved closer, and a mother raccoon and baby, eyes circled like bandits wearing masks, crept up to the hole and looked down at her. Megan laughed in relief. Then she remembered reading that raccoon feces held some horrible bug and could cause paralysis and mental retardation. Blindness, too. Even death. In the article she'd read, a child had died after getting raccoon feces in a cut. What if raccoon feces in the mud was getting right into her open wound? This place gave her the creeps.

"Get!" she shouted. "Get!"

The raccoons drew back. The mother pushed the baby in front of her as they made for the safety of the trees. Megan sighed, feeling mean. They hadn't meant to hurt her. They couldn't help being raccoons. She heard a loud shuffling noise. Was that Sydney? Was it the poachers? The noise grew louder, and a big, black, hairy snout poked over the roots at the top of the hole, followed by two tiny, gleaming red eyes. A wild boar. Megan cringed. The boar peered down into the hole, nostrils quivering. She could hear its heavy breathing. It began stomping its hooves slowly. Was it going to attack? She let out a shriek.

Something furry launched itself from the nearby tree, landing right beside her. Baby Furball, fur bristling, pulled himself erect and screamed wildly again and again, his mouth wide open and his teeth bared. Startled, the boar snorted twice and turned away, charging into the trees.

"You saved me, Baby!"

Tears streaming down her cheeks, Megan flung her arms around the little animal. She was so glad he was back. "Now, if only you could help me get out of here . . ."

She drew her knees up, shielding the broken leg, and curled her body around the warm little orangutan. Her leg throbbed, and her lips and eyes felt as if they'd been glued shut. She buried her face in the red fur and thought of her bedroom back home.

How she wished she were there. She pictured the quilted silver bedcover, the white curtains blowing gently in the breeze, her posters—the sleek black panther, the wolf peering from behind snow-laden trees, the lion cubs—

and her cats, Midnight and Simba. She'd found them when they were kittens, left at the side of the road in a shoebox. She'd fed them, dipping her finger in a powdered milk mixture again and again through long nights. She had rubbed their stomachs to help their digestion, wiped them with a damp cloth, been the mother cat they'd never known. And they'd not only lived but thrived. She smiled as she remembered them drinking their milk from doll's bottles, little paws holding on. She felt broken, like an old Barbie doll, one of the many she and Sydney had played with when they were young. They'd held Barbie jumping contests, throwing the poor dolls over the balcony. They'd given all the dolls different personalities. Ken, the boy, had been a bit of a dork. What a relief it would be to see nice, fresh-faced Ken appear now. Or even Luke's old G.I. Joe.

Wouldn't that be a relief!

Marianne, her first doll, was the only Barbie left. She sat on the corner of her desk, smothered by CDs and makeup—a much nicer sight than these skeletons and bones. Marianne was the meanest Barbie but also the most resourceful. She'd triumphed in every game. What would Marianne do if she were here now? Marianne would never be lost in a pit. Never! But then Marianne was a doll, and her anklebone wasn't broken. Megan shuddered and started to pray.

CHAPTER 17

Adam sat up reluctantly. He shivered. It was cold without Sydney's body clinging to his. They'd been lying, pressed together, on the back seat of the boat. It hadn't exactly been comfortable, but the kissing was amazing. He wished he could just keep lying there.

The bay stretched in front of them, looking gray and choppy and immense. He didn't like the thought of crossing it, but to go around the banks would take days. He didn't like the look of the dark clouds, either—he'd had enough storms.

"We'd better go," he said.

Sydney groaned.

"I know." He stroked her shoulder. "That's how I feel, too, but we need to move while it's dark."

He grabbed an oar and shoved at the bank, and the boat moved out into the deeper water. He passed the oar to Sydney and firmly grasped the makeshift pole he'd made.

"Okay. We'll have to try to do this together. Sing some sort of rowing song or something."

"Can I say a poem for help?" Sydney asked.

"Sure. We could use it."

Digging her oar into the water, she began to recite: "Hear me, four quarters of the world—a relative I am! Give me the strength to walk the soft earth, a relative to all that is! Give me the eyes to see and the strength to understand, that I may be like you. With your power only can I face the winds."

"Wow," Adam said, his eyes shining. "That's from *Black Elk Speaks*, isn't it?"

"Yes," Sydney nodded, looking shy.

"It's a Sioux Indian prayer," Adam said softly. "Thank you."

They poled on, slowly pulling the awkward airboat across the water in a wavering line. The bay was shallow, the depths sometimes as low as four feet. Sneaking a peek at Sydney, Adam smiled to himself. Imagine her quoting from *Black Elk Speaks*! That was one of his favorite poems. He felt in a daze as he moved along, trying to keep up a steady rhythm; and, already, his arms and shoulders ached. He needed to tap a bit farther into his Indian heritage, he thought. In the Indian Wars of the 1800s, his people, the Miccosukee, were noted for their courage and were proud to call themselves unconquered.

Sydney rubbed her shoulders.

"I'll pole alone for a while," Adam said. "You have a rest. Pretend we're on a gondola."

For a while, Sydney sat back, eyes closed, and she woke with a start. She'd actually fallen asleep. Adam still stood there, poling. She looked at him anxiously. "You've been poling for ages. Let me try."

"Not now. We have to get help as fast as possible."

"We're still miles from the campground. Come on, Adam. You'll be able to go faster if you rest a bit."

She stood up, struggling to keep her balance and to keep hold of the oar. Lips pressed together with determination, she pushed hard into the mud. The boat moved sluggishly forward. She pushed harder. The thing was heavy, much more difficult to move than she'd imagined. Adam had his eyes closed. At least he was getting a rest. Though at the rate she was poling, they'd soon be going backward. Set on doing better, she leaned all of her weight against the oar. The boat moved sluggishly forward. A large log bobbed toward them. She pushed hard, trying to avoid hitting it, and yelled as the prow jammed right into it. Adam sat up with a start.

"Sorry," Sydney said.

"It's okay." He smiled at her. "A few bumps, but at least you haven't sunk us yet." He put his hands behind his head and lay back, looking as if he was enjoying the ride.

Dipping the oar into the water, Sydney splashed him. "Thanks," she said. "Actually, I'm getting a bit better at it."

Adam watched her as she poled along, wisps of hair

falling into her eyes as her tanned, slightly muscled arms moved rhythmically. Her face glowed red with exertion. Behind the strange, mud-based eye makeup, her eyes shown electric blue. He smiled to himself. Syd looked like an Amazonian warrior woman. She'd been so nervous, yet she was the one who'd freed Megan.

"Sydney," he said. "When we get back, and this is all over, I want to take you and Megs and Luke to my favorite beach. It's a cove near Key West with powder-white sand. You'll love it. There are Key deer there—special, tiny ones that peek through the pine trees."

"That'll be fun." Sydney paused and wiped the sweat from her eyes.

A cold wind whipped the surface of the bay into choppy waves. Thunder threatened in the distance, and jagged flashes of lightning played across the horizon. Adam watched the boat for signs of splitting. It creaked, sometimes hitting the muddy bank with a resounding thud.

"I hope this thing doesn't sink," Sydney said. "It sure beats walking."

Another inlet appeared ahead. Adam reached for the oar. The boat was full of pieces of fish, and Sydney, sliding back down onto a seat, grimaced at the sight of blood and fish parts sloshing around her legs. Reaching for the plastic bag, she began scooping the water, bone, and gristle and tossing it overboard.

"Hey!" Adam said. "Don't do that! You'll attract sharks."

"You're the one rubbing a shark's tooth."

Self-conscious, Adam let go of the shark's tooth hanging on a thin leather strip around his neck. "Perhaps I'm calling a shark spirit to help us," he said.

"Please don't," Sydney said.

A shark fin slashed through the water. Horrified and breathing shallowly, they stared as the sinister black shape cruised around the side of the boat. It moved fast, gliding through the water, much more in charge of this territory than they were. Adam's heart began to pound, and his arms shook. Cold sweat formed on his skin. This shark was huge; the black shadow cruising beside them looked ten feet long. Would it try to turn over the boat? Could it? Suddenly, the shark made a sharp, tight turn and swam away as quickly as it had come.

"Wow! That was scary!" Sydney gasped. "Does it know we're in the boat? Does it want to eat us?"

"No," Adam said. "It wasn't attacking us. It was just curious."

"Okay, so it doesn't know we're here? It can't smell us or sense us or anything?"

"No. Well, at least I don't think so."

Hands clasped together, they peered into the black water. There was a violent bang. The boat rocked. Adam and Sydney tumbled from their seats to the floor, clinging to whatever they could.

"Go away!" Adam yelled, thumping the bottom of the boat. "Go away! Get!" The fin appeared again, rising in a black silhouette from the water. The shark circled. Adam thrust the oar in the direction of the fin, slamming into the shark's back.

"Don't make him mad, Adam," Sydney whimpered. The shark smashed into the boat with another blow. Then, as suddenly as it came, it disappeared, leaving Adam and Sydney shaken and feeling as if they'd been attacked by a gang of hoodlums.

"That was like *Jaws*," Sydney said. "I thought you said it was friendly."

"It wasn't that friendly," Adam said. Every little slap of wave was making him jump, ready to resume the fight. Then the storm joined the battle as the sky opened and rain poured down. Waves from the bay streamed into the inlet, turning the boat like a leaf in the current.

"We're going to sink, Adam," Sydney cried. "I'll never be able to swim here. I'll drown!"

Adam poled as hard as he could. Trying to reach a quiet haven, he headed down the inlet and back to the maze of canals. It was dark now and hard to see where he was going. Flashes of lightning silhouetted the trees. The small boat tossed and lurched through the churning water. Soaked and shivering, they reached the mangrove shore, where a final wave tipped the boat and knocked them into the mud. Scrambling up the bank, they peered into the darkness of swamp and mangroves.

CHAPTER 18

The rain had stopped, and a full moon appeared from behind the clouds. On the nearest hammock, a shack balanced precariously on crooked black stilts. Faint yellow light shone through the windows, like Halloween eyes gleaming in the dark.

"We'll go closer and see if anyone's there," Adam said.

"At least we can telephone for help," Sydney said.

"They probably don't have phones here," Adam replied.

"But they have electricity," Sydney said.

"No, they probably have kerosene lamps. The people living in the swamplands don't have much at all."

They climbed back into the boat and poled it along the shoreline toward the shack. Adam caught Sydney's arm and pointed at a small motorboat tied to a dilapidated dock. "We may be in luck," he whispered, tying the airboat next to the boat. "Stay here. Some of these people don't like strangers. I'll go and see who lives here. Looks like a family; there's a kid's bike over there. Got to be a good sign. Lie flat in the boat so they can't see you. If they seem all right, I'll call you."

As he walked up the path, the front door swung open and a small child walked out onto the porch. She had a narrow, pretty face and long, pale blonde hair that gleamed in the moonlight. She stared up at Adam.

"Hullo." Adam smiled at her. "Where's your mom? Can you get her for me?"

The child wiped her dripping nose on her hand, gave him one more long look, and ran back into the house, banging the door behind her. Adam looked back in Sydney's direction and shrugged. He turned and knocked on the door. Silence. He knocked again. "Hullo, is anyone there?"

The door opened a crack, and a tall, thin woman with pale blonde hair wearing a faded blue dress peeked out. "What do you want?"

Adam smiled as politely as he could. He hoped he wasn't frightening them. "I need to get some help. I want to contact the park rangers. Do you have a telephone?"

"No," the woman replied flatly.

"Can you help me get back to the campground at Flamingo? I'm lost."

The woman said nothing. She just stood there. Adam wondered if there was something wrong with her. Then she opened the door wider and motioned him to come inside.

Sydney waited and waited, moving restlessly in the boat. She was tired of crouching beside the seat, and she needed to pee. She could see a ramshackle, small building near the back of the house and guessed it was the toilet. It looked uninviting, dirty, and old. She decided she'd rather find a place in the bushes she could use. As she surveyed the scene around the dock, she kept a watch out for Adam. He was taking a long time.

Feeling an itch on her leg, she brushed at it and touched something slimy. She pulled her fingers away fast and stared down at her leg. A leech! It was about three inches long and attached to her skin. Oh yuck! Grimacing, she tried to pull it off, but it clung, hard, to her flesh. She shuddered. How could she get it off? She needed something sharp.

She climbed out of the boat, into the stagnant water, and up the bank. Iron and metal contraptions of various shapes were outlined in the moonlight, littering the dirt around the house. With dismay, she realized what they were. Animal traps! So these people were also into trapping animals.

A rusty knife lay next to a trap. She grabbed it and lifted the leech, cutting it in two, and pulled at the head. It came away with a sickening suck. Sydney shuddered again but firmly held onto the knife. A thick metal rod with a jagged edge lay near her feet, and she picked that up, too. With a weapon in each hand, she stood with her feet apart and took a deep breath. She was tired of being attacked; she was going to attack back. She wasn't going to scream, cry, or give up ever again. She was an Amazon woman on the warpath. Yeah!

The shack door creaked open, and she sighed in relief, expecting to see Adam, but she sank back into the saw grass when a fair-haired child appeared. Then two tall teenagers, with the same long, fly-away blond hair as the child, appeared from behind the shack. The tallest, a tough-looking character, held a rifle he swung back and forth as they strode toward the shack. Metal shone in the moonlight.

Sydney ducked down. There wasn't a sound from the house and Adam didn't appear. Something was wrong.

Feeling awkward, Adam stood at the entrance of the small living room. He'd known these backwoods people might not be hospitable, but this lot was weird. Both the woman and the little girl stared at him. Neither said a word.

The inside of the shack was even more dilapidated than the outside, but it looked cozy enough in the light of the lamp. The room was furnished with a tattered sofa, covered with a worn green blanket, and a rocking chair. A lopsided table and four dining room chairs stood in the far corner next to a wood stove. A pot of fish stew simmered on the stove, and a bowl on the table was filled with corn bread. It smelled delicious. Adam heard his stomach begin to growl, sounding like it had spotted the food and was about to spring on it. He wished they would offer him something.

Nervous, he cleared his throat. "Could I have some water, please?"

The woman nodded at the child, who walked backward out the door, not taking her eyes off him. Did he look so bad that he was scary? He pushed back his long hair. Maybe they were afraid of him. A pump handle squeaked, and the child came back, carrying a broken mug full of water. He gulped it down. He wondered if he should get Sydney. Surely these people weren't a threat. If he could persuade them to lend them the motorboat at the dock, at least he and Sydney could get to the campground tonight. But the boat was no doubt their only means of transport, and they wouldn't want to part with it.

"My friend and I are lost," he said, trying to speak slowly and clearly. "We got caught in a storm, and our boat was wrecked. I need to get back to the campground at Flamingo. Could we please borrow your boat? My parents will pay you."

The woman just looked silently at him.

"I need your help," Adam said slowly and firmly. "Two of my friends are hurt. They're out there in the swamps. And there are poachers out there. Bad men. I have to get help fast. My uncle is a park ranger."

The woman's eyes narrowed as she looked at him, and she nodded. She motioned to the little girl and pointed to the door. Adam stood, waiting. He didn't know what was happening or what else to say. Why was the mother sending her child back outside? Had she decided to help him? He wanted their help more than he'd ever wanted anything in his life.

"Look"—he held out his arm—"You can have my watch and hold it until I return the boat. I got it for my birthday. It's new. It's a Swatch."

The door opened again, and he heard a movement behind him. He turned around expecting to see the child. A hard blow landed on his head. Seeing stars, he reeled, trying to recover his balance, but fell to the floor. With effort, he managed to stand up and stagger in the direction of the door, but another blow landed at the base of his neck.

He crashed to the floor, unconscious.

CHAPTER 19

Adam opened his eyes. His head ached, and when he gingerly felt it, he found a big, egg-shaped bump. Groaning, he tried to work out what else was wrong. He was trussed up like some captured animal, his arms and legs tied together and secured to the legs of a solid, wooden, four-poster bed. The ropes were tight, and his arms and legs throbbed.

Trying to free himself, he strained his back to push up the bed, but it was too heavy to budge. He heard a muffled grunt and a noise. What was that? He peered under the bed. Two blue eyes peered back at him. Luke! Luke was tied to the other side of the bed. Duct tape covered his mouth, and he was making a soft grunting sound, almost like a chimpanzee.

Adam couldn't say a word; his mouth was too tightly taped. He nodded his head furiously at Luke and winked. Luke winked back enthusiastically. Adam began to struggle, working to free the ropes on his wrists. This only made them tighter, however, and pins and needles began to run up and down his arms.

He lay still as he heard voices from the other room. He listened intently.

"Jed, you have to fetch Sam," the woman said. "Tell him we have another kid. I don't want them here. It's trouble."

"What's Uncle Sam going to do to them?" The little girl had a high, whining voice.

"Probably going to off them," a man's voice said. "His boss is mad. The whole thing's going nuts, and he doesn't want the law coming after him."

"Probably going to hunt them first." The guy called Jed gave a high-pitched giggle. "Sam's boss is crazy."

"Yeah, Boss Man Frank loves going a-hunting. He did that before, when that nosy tourist guy came snooping around. That guy's body turned up in the swamp. Folks said an alligator got him. But it was Frank that got him first."

"Yeah!" Jed sounded happier by the minute. "Hey, he could let them loose on the island, and we could all go after them. Frank and all the guys. Have a prize for the winner."

"They belong to Frank," the mother said. "You'll have to let Sam know so he can call Frank. Frank will deal with it."

"I'll go in the morning," Jed replied. "I'm beat. Frank's going to just love my idea."

Adam could hear them slurping the stew with relish, and his stomach growled like an attack dog. He looked at Luke, who widened his eyes and grimaced. How could they get away from here?

There were sounds of shuffling, low voices, and then the lamp went off. Soon, the house was silent and dark. Adam knew Sydney would come for him. Already, he could picture her creeping up the path, and his heart beat furiously with fear for her. But what if she didn't come? What if she decided to take the motorboat and tried to get to the Flamingo campground alone?

Could she manage that? She'd probably get lost in the Glades. And what if she met up with good old Frank? He tugged at his bonds and decided that the best bet would be to lift the bed. If he managed that, he could slide the ropes free. He rolled his legs over in Luke's direction and kicked at him to get his attention. Then he placed his shoulder under the bed and began pushing to lift it. Luke immediately got the idea. He began pushing up from the other side.

Bracing their backs under the heavy frame, they both pushed steadily at the bed until it lifted an inch into the air. Adam gritted his teeth, taking the full weight as Luke wiggled down and slid his arms and feet clear. His face red with effort, Luke held up the bed frame while Adam did the same. Then, as two silent, trussed shadows, they rolled together and maneuvered their backs to each other, and

Adam began struggling to untie the rope on Luke's wrists.

He was still working at the knot when he heard a soft tap on the window. Sydney! She waved, eyes shining with relief at seeing Adam and Luke. Wiggling a knife blade between the window frame and the sill, she freed the latch. The window creaked.

Adam heard loud footsteps running across the other room. He dived to the floor and lay close to the bed, his eyes closed. He hoped Luke had the presence of mind to do the same. The door burst open. Peeping out from under his lashes, Adam could see the women and the two teenagers. One of the teens was big and tough-looking, the other tall and skinny. The light from the woman's kerosene lamp flicked back and forth as she moved it nervously around.

"What's going on here?" she shouted. "Look! They're loose! Can't you lazy louts even tie someone up properly?"

She kicked Adam hard. He groaned as pain shot through his ribs. "Check the other one," she shouted. "You stupid idiots! These kids were about to escape. Frank would kill us. Get the needle. It's safer if we put them out."

Tough Guy grabbed Adam and began roughly twisting the rope around his wrists again. Adam struggled free and managed to get to his knees, but Tough Guy, grinning, shoved him back to the floor. He heard the crack as his head hit the bed. Spots of light appeared before his eyes, and his head hummed. He pulled himself back up, staggering, trying to kick and thrust at his attacker. Luke jumped up and made a dash for the door. Skinny Guy tackled him, flinging him back to the ground.

"I said get the needle," the woman shouted at the little girl. "Hurry!"

The child began to cry. "I don't want you to stick him with the needle. When Uncle Sam stuck the monkeys with the needle, they died. I saw them, and they were dead."

"You do as I say, and do it now," the woman said. "Move!"

Adam lay, half-conscious, on the floor. Dimly, he saw the woman kneeling over him. Her pale, long face faded in and out. Tough Guy held his arms as she stuck a long hypodermic needle into a bottle and filled the vial with a gray liquid. Cold sweat beaded his forehead. The point of the needle was encrusted with blood. There was no way he was going to let that thing into his arm! With whatever strength he could find, he pushed, kicked, and pulled away.

"Hold him tighter," the woman said. "I need to get that vein."

"Give it to me." Tough Guy grabbed the needle with one hand and bent over Adam. Adam grabbed his wrist and pulled him sideways and forward. The needle jammed in the floor. The guy swore. As he made a grab for the needle, Adam kicked, scoring a hard one to the guy's nose. The guy backed off for a moment, and Adam took his chance, grabbing the needle and holding it like a weapon before his chest. "Anybody want a piece of it?" he shouted.

With a roar of anger, Tough Guy pulled himself up and lunged at Adam again. Adam fell backward on the floor as the guy crashed down on him, swinging his fists.

They landed with a thud, and then the guy shrieked and drew back. Stunned, Adam saw the needle buried in the guy's chest.

Tough Guy began whimpering, staring at the needle.

Adam reached out, shocked. He was about to try to help, to pull the needle out or something, when Skinny Guy lunged at him, sending him crashing back down again.

"Get back. Leave him alone." Adam heard Sydney's nervous, high-pitched voice before he saw her. His heart thudded furiously. Oh God! Sydney! Now they'd get her, too.

"Get away from here, Sydney!" he shouted. His attacker let go of his head, and he managed to look up. Sydney stood in the doorway, clutching a large hunting rifle, her finger pressed to the trigger.

"Get off him," she shouted. "I'll shoot you if you don't. I'm a wild shot. I don't know where I'll shoot you, and I don't care, either. If I kill you, it's too bad. Get away from him, all of you, and stick your hands above your heads."

The woman and the two guys stood up slowly, backing toward the wall, hands above their heads. Tough Guy groaned.

"Don't move!" Sydney shouted. "Adam! Luke! Are you okay? Can you tie them up?"

Adam felt his mouth widening into a huge grin. He couldn't control it. Or maybe it wasn't really a grin. Maybe he was going to cry.

Luke scrambled to his feet, shoved his attacker over

onto his back, and began to tie him up with the ropes he and Adam had just removed.

"You'll need some rope for the others," Sydney said. "Cut that piece in half. There's a knife in my belt." Sydney stood, pointing the rifle at their captors. "Cut the lamp cord. You can rope the woman with that."

Adam gaped at her. "You've turned into some sort of Wonder Woman!"

Sydney smiled. Wonder Woman? Yeah, she liked the feeling. "Quickly," she said. "Finish tying this lot. We'll take their motorboat and their rifles and get out of here. And I guess you should pull the needle out of that guy's chest, Adam. But make sure he's tied up first!"

Luke whooped in triumph as they left the room. Adam stopped. The little girl was cowering under the table. He reached toward her, and she shrank back.

"Hey, it's okay. We're not going to hurt you," he said. "We didn't hurt your mom or brothers, either. Your brother will be okay. You can untie them, you know. Just wait a little while until we're gone. Okay?"

The child stared at him.

"We're going to help the poor animals your Uncle Sam has," Adam said.

Eyes focused on Adam, the little girl crawled out slowly and backed into the kitchen. Adam, Luke, and Sydney followed.

"Hey, that corn bread looks good," Adam said.

Wiping the tears from her eyes, the child reached into the bowl and pulled out a handful of corn bread. She handed it to Adam.

"Thank you," he said. "Just wait a little before you let them loose, okay? We're taking your boat, but I promise we'll get it back to you."

The little girl nodded. She watched them as they headed for the boat. Adam turned and waved, and hesitantly, the child waved back.

Adam set the throttle for the outboard motor, pulled out the choke, and gave a pull on the starter. The motor coughed. Sydney held her breath. He tapped the choke in to get the propeller turning, and with a roar, the small boat headed out into the creek. With one hand, Sydney clutched the seat, and with the other, she clutched Luke. "I can't believe we're all together. I wish Megs was with us. How long will it take us to get help, Adam?"

"We have the rifle and Wonder Woman with her weapons!" he grinned at Sydney. "We can rescue Megs ourselves—we don't need anyone's help."

"Yes!" Sydney said. She looked across the bay and willed the boat faster over the water. "We're coming, Megs! We're coming!"

Adam placed the gun carefully in the storage bench, and they roared off across the dark Florida Bay.

CHAPTER 20

Megan shivered. How weird that she was in the steamy Everglades and she'd never been colder in her life. Thick mist covered the Glades. Another great day, she thought. If she was lucky enough to get out of here alive, she'd certainly have a "different" vacation story to tell. Suddenly, she remembered it was Halloween, her favorite night of the year. What a place to spend Halloween! Couldn't beat the atmosphere.

She thought of her worried dad and sniffed back a sob. He'd always tagged a few paces behind when she, Sydney, and Luke went trick-or-treating. Two years ago, she'd told him she and Sydney were much too old to ask for candy, but he'd looked so disappointed that they'd ended up going anyway. She'd dressed as a vampire, and

Sydney had dressed as Princess Leia. They'd come back with tons of candy and dumped their booty on the kitchen table. Then they'd fought for hours about who'd get to eat the Snickers. How she'd love a Snickers now.

Then last year she'd gone to a Goth Halloween party. That had been way cool—well, for a while anyway, until she'd done a totally embarrassing thing. She'd dressed up to look astonishingly bad: a great, wispy white bridal dress from a thrift store, black nail polish, and lipstick. She'd put the black lipstick on after she'd left the house so her parents wouldn't freak. The party was in someone's basement. She didn't know the girl well, but she'd been thrilled to be invited. And all the undead there were so friendly, so fun. She'd been wide-eyed and eager to impress. For reasons she still wasn't clear about, she'd grabbed the fire extinguisher, aimed it at a guy she thought was cute, and squirted it. Her only excuse was she'd thought the fire extinguisher was a fake. Bad mistake. It wasn't.

The guy had turned white. He was sort of a solid type, so he'd looked like the Pillsbury Doughboy Dracula. And then he was coughing and spluttering. Turned out he had bad asthma. It was pretty much the end of the party.

The girl's parents drove her home, all tight-lipped and silent, and her parents were furious. How on Earth could she do a thing like that, they'd asked her again and again. But the next day, at school, the Goths had still been really nice. In fact, they thought the whole thing was a blast. How she wished she could see a nice Goth friend right about now.

She felt shaky from lack of food and water. Was that why she lay here dreaming, thinking of the past? Was she losing it? How long could a person live without water? Ten days? She remembered reading that somewhere. She'd given up the hope of being rescued, and she didn't even want to think about what had happened to the others. She hoped they weren't all dead, killed by the poachers' bullets. She pushed the thought from her mind. Sydney, Luke, and Adam—she was the idiot who'd brought them all into this horrible adventure. The thought made her feel totally sick.

Flies swarmed around her, and Baby Furball caught them one by one and popped them into his mouth. "Yuck! Don't eat those," she said, pulling him closer. He looked intently at her, reached up, caught a few more flies, and squashed them in his hand. Then he offered them to her. "Thanks, but no thanks!" She patted his head. She felt so close to the little animal. She was so miserable, and he was all she had. What would happen to him if she died in this hole?

She decided to make one last desperate attempt to pull herself out. Placing her weight on her broken ankle would be agonizing, but dying would be worse. If she managed to get out, she could make a crutch from some branches and hobble to the shelter. There, at least she'd have some food and water. Tentatively, she tried to stand, and a sharp flash of pain shot up her leg. She shrieked and clutched her leg, whimpering. "I've got to do it, or I'm going to die in this hole, and no one will ever know." She looked back at the small white monkey bones and pictured her bones lying there, too.

She heard a crackling noise. Someone was coming through the bushes. "Sydney!" she called. "Sydney, I'm here in this hole."

A wavering cone of yellow light darted around in the trees. Megan froze. Sydney didn't have a flashlight.

Then she heard a high-pitched giggle, and a voice said, "Boo!"

Megan started. Who was this?

"Great place to be. Couldn't have picked it better myself."

Megan stared, speechless. The movie-star poacher stood at the top of the hole, leering down at her. He still looked somewhat like Leonardo, but this time he belonged in a horror movie. The torchlight lit his face, turning his eyes into ghoulish holes, creating dark, Dracula-like hollows in his cheeks.

"Spooky in the woods at night, isn't it?" He giggled, as if he'd made some hilarious joke.

Megan slid to the far side of the hole, trying to get as far away from him as possible.

"That was a nasty thing you did," he said. "You and your friends have cost me a lot of money."

Megan nodded. She was glad she'd cost him a lot of money, but it didn't seem like a good time to say so.

She realized the man wasn't looking at her. His gaze was fixed at a place over her shoulder. A strange smile formed on his face.

"It's Halloween, you know," he said. "Trick or treat?

You look like the type of girl who gets into Halloween. Guess you want a real treat. What do you think about your very own snake? A nice big one, a water moccasin or something?"

What was he staring at? Megan looked around and gasped. A very large snake was slithering down into the hole, heading right in her direction. She slid as fast as she could away from the creature and reached up for the poacher's help. "It's coming right at me! Get me out of here," she screamed.

"Maybe if you say please," the man said.

"Please. Please. Please get me out of here."

"Are you kidding?" the man grinned nastily, showing his tiny white teeth. "What did you ever do for me? But I'll do you a favor and give you some advice: you'd better stay really still. Snakes sense movement. Let's see how good you are at playing dead."

He leaned over the top of the hole, and Megan saw his gleeful smile. Mesmerized, she watched the snake slither closer. Should she try to hit it? No, it could strike faster than she could. "Please, please pull me out of here," she whimpered.

The man smiled and watched, his eyes glowing with excitement. The snake lifted its head, and its yellow eyes moved back and forth as it searched in the moonlight for the slightest movement. It slid closer. Megan froze, hardly breathing. It was so close, she could see the individual scales on its back. Fur raised, Baby Furball clutched at her arm.

"It can smell you!" The man chuckled. "Wow, so cool!"

The snake reared up. As it drew back its head, its mouth opened wide, showing sharp fangs. Its head swung back and forth in a slow, hypnotic movement. It was going to strike!

Megan held her breath. Time seemed to stop. The snake dropped its head and slid closer. Sick with horror, she felt its hard, cold body, its muscles flexing, slide past her outstretched leg. The injured leg. The leg with the blood. Could it smell the blood? Surely it could hear her heart pounding. Was this what a heart attack felt like? She stayed as still as if she were already dead.

Then the snake slithered down, back into the mud, and away from her.

"Man, that was a trip!" the man said. "Could have killed you easily."

Megan stared at him. Was he insane? Baby Furball came crawling out from behind Megan and raised himself up into a standing position, shrieking at the man.

"You've got the orangutan!" he exclaimed.

"You're not going to get him." Megan hugged the small animal. Baby Furball whimpered.

"Oh, and who is going to stop me? I'm certainly going to get him. And most of the other animals. This is an island. They've got to be here somewhere. Sam and Buddy are looking for them now, and they're pretty motivated. Do you realize what those animals are worth?" He smiled. "I love this kind of work. Never a dull moment. We have your friend. He's up at Sam's sister's house. Maybe I'll bring him to join you. Good place for the two of you. Nice little mudhole. And if you escape, my guys and I can hunt you." He looked thoughtful. "Another manhunt. I could give you an hour's chance to get away, and then off we go."

Megan felt sick.

"Give me that ape," he ordered. "Pass him over to me."

Megan clung to Baby Furball, who wrapped his arms around her neck.

"If you make me come and get that ape, you'll be very sorry. Push him up to me now, and I'll help you out."

Megan clutched the orangutan tighter, and he burrowed his head into her shoulder.

Fury flashed across the man's face. "Okay, I'll get him myself." He took off his leather jacket and hung it carefully on a branch.

A sudden noise, like that of loud monkey gibbering, came from the bushes on the far side of the hole. "The gibbons!" he said. "Great! The gibbons are right here!"

There was a dull thud.

Then, to Megan's total shock, the poacher grunted, lurched toward her, tottered at the edge of the hole like an off-balance tightrope walker, and tumbled headfirst into the mud, landing facedown at her feet.

"Yesss! I got him! Yes! Yes!" Adam appeared at the top of the hole, whooping and doing a war dance, stomping in the mud and waving the rifle.

And there was Sydney, at his side, bending down as far as she could and reaching out. "Megs, are you all right?"

"Yes, almost." Megan gulped. She couldn't believe she was seeing them.

"Great gibbon noises, Luke," Adam called.

Luke appeared, grinning widely and looking pleased with himself. "Great head-butting with that rifle!"

Sydney frowned. "Why are you sitting like that, Megs? What's wrong with your leg?"

"Let's get out of here," Megan said. "We don't know where the other two creeps are, and I'd rather not find out. My ankle's broken. My whole leg's a mess. You'll have to help me."

Megan shrieked as the poacher dived across the mud and grabbed her broken ankle. "Adam!" she screamed. "Adam!"

"Let go of her!" Adam shouted, pointing the rifle at the man.

With a twisted grin, the poacher looked up at Adam and lifted Megan's leg, thumping it down hard on the ground. She shrieked with pain. "Stupid, idiotic damn kids," he shouted. "Throw that rifle down here."

"No way," Adam gripped the rifle, his arms trembling and his eyes wide. "Let her go. I'll fire this if you don't."

"No, you won't," the poacher said. "You don't even know how to, do you? Never fired a gun in your sucking, little, pampered life. Besides, I've got this."

He pulled a gun out of his belt and fired. Rocks and roots shattered, and Adam and Luke jumped back. "Throw down that rifle now," he shouted. "This is a Colt forty-five. Small gun but it makes nice, big holes."

Grabbing Megan's ankle again, he twisted it savagely and she screamed, tears running down her cheeks. "Shoot him, Adam," she shouted. "Shoot him!"

"Oh yeah," the poacher mimicked, raising his voice. "'Shoot him!'" He fired again. Adam jumped to the side and screamed in shock as the bullet grazed his arm, leaving bright, fresh streaks of blood. He dropped the rifle, then grasped for it blindly as it bounced on the ground and slid down the first few feet of the slough hole.

Her face red with fury, Sydney ran to the side of the hole and jumped, clutching the crowbar and the knife. She landed behind the poacher, lifted the crowbar, and brought it down hard, missing his head but landing a blow between his shoulders and his neck. For a minute, he slid backward into the mud, but then, clawing at the roots, he pulled himself up into a sitting position and turned, thrusting the gun right into her face.

Screaming as she rolled forward in the slime, Megan fastened her fingers around a monkey skull and smashed it furiously, repeatedly, at the poacher's head. He turned back to her, and she crammed the skull into his nose as hard as she could. As he shouted and fell back, Sydney jumped up and slammed the crowbar onto his head.

"Stop! Stop! You'll kill him." Adam slid down the bank and grabbed the crowbar. Sydney waved the knife wildly, then dropped it, and flung herself into his arms, sobbing.

"Let's get out of here," Megan groaned, clutching her now-limp ankle. Baby Furball cringed beside her, whimpering and staring around with wide, fearful eyes. "We've made a lot of noise. The other men may be coming."

Gently, Adam picked up the small orangutan. "Everything's going to be okay, little guy," he said, passing him to Sydney. He winced as he looked at Megan's ankle. Taking off his shirt, he wrapped it around the broken bone. "That looks bad. Moving is going to hurt."

Megan slid away, out of the reach of the unconscious poacher, half expecting him to jump up again. She looked around wildly for the gun. "I'm okay. Just help me get out of here! Can you see the gun? Should we take the gun?"

"Just worry about getting out of there," Luke called.

"Adam!" Sydney cried. "You've been hit. Look at your arm. It's bleeding all over. You have to bandage that."

"I'll be okay," Adam said. "Get my arm shot at all the time."

Sydney grabbed his shoulder to see the wound, but he gently pushed her away. "No, really, Sydney, I'm okay. It's just a graze. We've got to get out of here. Those other men could arrive any minute."

Sliding down into the slough hole, Adam lifted Megan carefully and pushed her up the bank. Luke and Sydney grabbed her arms and pulled, heaving her out of the hole.

"Watch out for my ankle!" Megan cried. Shaking, she put her arms over Adam and Luke's shoulders and took a deep breath of relief. At least she was out of the hole from hell. She looked back at the motionless body in the mud. There was no sign of the gun, and she didn't want to take time searching for it. "Bye-bye, creep," she shouted. "Maybe that eight-foot-long rattlesnake will come back and entertain you again."

She held out her arms to Baby Furball, but he stuck his head into Sydney's shoulder and shrieked.

"What's up, dude?" Megan said. "Don't tell me you'd rather stay with Sydney."

Then she heard the strange rattling sound. "Adam! Listen! The snake! Where is it?"

Adam froze. He'd heard a rattlesnake's death rattle before—the snake was about to strike. Where was it? Frantically, he looked around. Where was the rattle coming from?

Megan spotted the rattlesnake first—the long, diamond-patterned body slowly uncoiling, the triangular head raised, the cold cat-like eyes focused on Sydney. "Don't move, Sydney!" she screamed. "It's behind you."

Sydney screeched and turned, dropping Baby Furball. She raised her hands in horror, fingers spread wide. The snake reared back. Adam dove, pushing her to the ground just feet from the snake. The rattlesnake struck, jamming its pointed teeth into Adam's arm.

Sydney screamed and grabbed the snake's tail. She pulled frantically until it let go of Adam and fell to the ground, jerking, its tongue pointing in and out.

"Get back! Get away from it!" Adam shouted. He clutched the bite, his face pale.

"Kill it!" Luke shouted, looking around wildly for a stick.

"Get away from it. It'll strike again." Adam stumbled down the track, then stopped and stared at his arm, examining it as if it didn't belong to him.

"We have to cut its head off," Luke said.

"Get away from it!" Adam groaned. "Move! Now!"

Megan leaned on Luke's shoulder, and they stumbled away from the snake. Sydney ran up to Adam, wrapping her arms around his shaking shoulders. "You're okay! You'll be okay! We'll get back to the camp. Your park ranger uncle will have antivenom."

Adam stared at the bite. Two holes showed clearly where the snake's teeth had pierced his skin. "Oh shit," he said. "It hurts. It's going to be a long time before we get to the camp. I want to get the poison out. Get my knife, Sydney. It's in my shirt pocket."

Megan fumbled for the knife. Sydney's hand shook as she took it. She crouched down beside Adam, staring at his arm and the red circle surrounding the bite. "How deep must I cut?"

Adam clutched his injured arm. "I don't know. I'm not sure if it's right to cut it."

"I think you're supposed to keep your arm still and get medical attention fast," Luke said.

"Yeah, what medical attention?"

"Wash it first," Megan said. "Wash the knife."

"There's an empty can in the boat. I'll get water." Luke ran ahead of them, somewhat awkwardly from his own injury, down to the creek. Megan, Sydney, and Adam stumbled together, with Megan wincing between them as they slowly followed after Luke.

"Careful," Luke said as he helped Megan into the boat, then Adam. Turning to Sydney, Luke passed her a bottle that sloshed when she grasped it.

Sydney poured water over the bite, wiping it gently with the edge of her shirt. Then she washed and wiped the knife. "This water's muddy," she said. Her face was pale, and her lips pressed together.

Adam closed his eyes. "Tie a sock above it. Not too tight. Then cut. You have to cut across the bite . . . I think."

Sydney clenched her teeth and started to cut. The knife was blunt. She grimaced and pushed harder, sawing slightly back and forth. Adam gasped sharply and clutched the seat, knuckles white. Bright red blood poured from his arm, over the seat, and onto the bottom of the boat, pooling around their feet. They watched, mesmerized, until the blood slowed.

"There'll still be poison in there. I'm going to suck it out," Sydney said.

"No, don't," Adam said. "I'm not sure if that's the right thing to do. It's got to be dangerous for you."

"I'm going to try. Just a bit. It'll be good to try to get some more out. Okay?" Sydney leaned over and placed her hands on each side of the bite.

"No!" Adam screamed. He closed his eyes and lay back, clutching his arm.

Sydney stared at his arm. "We need to get to the camp quickly. He needs a doctor."

Luke looked grim. "And we need him to find the way back to the campground. We won't find it without him."

CHAPTER 21

Luke started up the motorboat as Megan watched the small waves ripple out around them. Her leg throbbed as she twisted around, and she looked over the faces around her. We look like a bunch of soldiers returning from a really bad war, Megan thought. Her heart hammered. They were so close to getting away, but they were in trouble. Bad trouble. If they didn't make it back to help soon, Adam could die. And she knew that she was in terrible danger from an infection. She couldn't bear to look at her ankle, and the throbbing seemed to have taken over her whole body. Her leg felt hot. She was sure to have blood poisoning. She looked back and scanned the jungle. Where were the poachers?

"I don't know where you guys got this motorboat, but

I'm really glad you did," Luke called from the driver's seat.

"Lie down. Try not to move your arm," Luke said to Adam. "If you keep it still, it stops the poison from traveling."

Megan had no idea which way to go. In front of her was a mangrove labyrinth leading nowhere. She turned to Adam, who was lying down partly under the seat. "Adam?"

"Yeah."

"Which way? We don't know the way out of here."

"Follow the tide," Adam's face was beaded with sweat. He rubbed his forehead and took a deep breath. "I think it's going out to the bay. Then try to head west."

"But I don't know which way west is."

"The sun's rising in the east, so your shadow will be pointing west. It's rough, I know, but it's the best I can think of." Adam rolled to his side, holding on to his injured arm. "We might run into another boat. They'll be looking for us. We'll get back eventually."

Sydney put her arms around his shoulders, stroking him and watching his face, her eyes dark with fear.

"Just get us out of here," Megan said. "Sydney, can you steer? I can't. My leg is killing me. Don't worry, I'll watch out for Adam."

"Just don't let him die," Sydney said.

"I won't," Megan said. "If he does, we're all dead."

Sydney took the wheel from Luke and revved the motor, heading off through the winding canals, trying to follow the way the tide seemed to be flowing.

They'd been on the water for what seemed like an

hour when she heard the thudding. As she stared at the horizon, the canal opened up to wide, sparkling Florida Bay and the welcome sight of a big motorboat roaring toward them. With a wide grin, Sydney called to the others, "Look! We're okay! We're saved! There's a motorboat coming, a big one. From way over there, see?"

A big boat, thumping up and down as it crashed across the swells, made its way to them from across the bay. Waving and jumping up and down with excitement, Sydney hung on to the steering wheel. She could see the National Parks green circle on the bow of the boat. Everything was going to be okay! It must be Adam's uncle, the park ranger. Luke jumped up and down, yelling, "Over here! Over here!"

The boat roared up, stopping alongside in a flurry of white water. A broad-shouldered, dark-skinned man waved, grinning at them. "I can't believe it's you kids! Everyone's looking for you—Adam? What happened?"

"We need snake-bite antivenom," Sydney shouted. "Do you have any? Adam's been bitten."

The boat came closer. "What bit him?"

"I think a rattler. It made a rattling sound before biting. It was big and it had a white-and-gray crisscross pattern."

"How many punctures?"

Sydney studied Adam's arm. "Two."

"And swelling? Is the swelling spreading?"

Sydney checked again. "No, not much. It's red and swollen at the bite."

"Okay, good. That's a good sign."

"We cut it," Sydney said.

"Oh. Well, we don't really do that much," the man said. "Used to do it, though. People try lots of things."

Sydney shuddered.

Pulling up alongside, the man rummaged in his boat's locker and produced a Red Cross first aid box. He leaned out and tossed the box to Luke, who grabbed it. He pulled up close to their boat. "Okay, the antivenom's in the yellow box. There's a syringe in there, too. Fill it with ten ccs, and inject a little into a muscle. Do a few more injections around the bite. Are you okay with that?"

Sydney nodded shakily.

"That'll hold him, but we need to get him back to a camp doctor as quickly as possible. Follow me."

Passing the wheel over to Luke, Sydney grabbed the box and opened the lid of serum. What if she messed this up? She'd never injected anyone before, ever. "Help me, Megan," she said. What was wrong with her sister? Megan had slipped off the seat and crouched, with her face hidden, in the bottom of the boat. Sydney looked up. Could Adam's uncle somehow come and do the injecting? But he'd reversed his boat and was waiting, boat bobbing in the swell.

"Found it?" he shouted.

"Yes." Sydney took out the syringe.

Megan tapped lightly against the hull of the boat.

"What?" Holding the small yellow vial tightly, Sydney nervously filled the syringe. She looked down at her sister. Megan looked frantic. Omigod, what was wrong now? Deciding on first things first, she ignored Megan and, gritting her teeth, plunged the needle into Adam's arm. Anxiously, she watched his face for any reaction. He looked so bad: his face was a horrible gray color.

"Keep something tied above the bite," the man shouted. "Not tight. A sock or something. And keep his arm still."

"Okay, I'm going to do it now," Sydney shouted. "Thank you so, so much."

The man gave her a thumbs-up sign. "Any nausea, vomiting?"

"No," Sydney said.

"Sounds like a partial bite," he shouted. "Partial envenomation. If that was a full bite, he'd be much worse."

Sydney gave a thumbs-up back, smiling with relief. Megan thumped the bottom of the boat.

"What's wrong with you?" Sydney said. "Can you please just help me? Sit up, will you?"

"That guy is one of the poachers," Megan hissed, keeping her head down. "If he sees me, it's over. He'll recognize me. He was right there in that shack."

"You're crazy!" Sydney stared over at the nearby boat. "That's not a poacher. He's Adam's uncle. He's a park ranger."

"Yeah, and his name is Buddy. I mean, how do you think I know his name? Be careful, and don't let on that we know."

"You're nuts." Sydney stood up, waving. "Okay! I injected it." She paused. A sick feeling ran through her. What if Megs was right? After all, she'd seen the poachers; she'd spoken to them. Taking a deep breath, she faked a smile and called out, "Are you Adam's Uncle Buddy?"

"You bet," the man shouted. "And don't worry—not too many deaths from rattlers, as long as the critter didn't bite right into a vein. Follow me, now. It's going to be a rough ride crossing the middle of the bay, but it's the fastest way back. Just follow in my wake. I'll move ahead so it won't rock you much."

Consider me rocked already, Sydney thought. She and Luke stared at Megan.

She shrugged, keeping her head down low. "Told you. Let him pull ahead. If he works this one out before we get back, we're finished."

"But he seems so nice," Sydney groaned. She snuck a quick look at Adam. Had he heard what Megan said? Maybe not. Eyes closed, he lay curled up with his head under the seat. What would he make of this? He'd sounded so proud of his uncle.

"Yeah, nice like a rattler," Megan said. "He won't be so nice if he realizes we're the kids his poacher friends are looking for. How long before that bombshell's going to hit?"

"I think it's hitting about now," Luke said. "He's slowing down and looking back at us."

Megan shouted, "Turn the boat around! Head back to the canals."

Whipping the wheel, Luke spun the boat. "His boat's faster. He'll get us real soon. Then what?"

CHAPTER 22

Pushing the engine to the max, they whipped back over the water toward the maze of islands. "Turn in!" Megan shouted. "Get into the mangroves."

Sydney twisted the wheel to the right, steering the small boat like some wild computer-game missile of destruction through the mangrove roots. Mud and water rose in plumes from the back and sides.

"Head for shallow water!"

"If we hit mud, we're dead."

"If he catches up to us, we're dead anyway. Move! Faster!"

"He won't kill us! He's Adam's uncle!"

"Yeah, and he knows we can put him in prison for a long time. Even if he doesn't want to kill us, I bet his boss,

Frank, would."

The large boat thundered after them, the roar from its engine growing louder by the second. They headed straight into a field of long saw grass, and the boat jerked and bounced as the bottom hit mud. Hands slick with water and mud, Sydney closed her eyes and clung to the wheel. They bumped down a shallow canal, mud flying. Spiky saw grass lashed their arms.

"Rev it! Rev the motor!" Megan shouted. "Get in there farther. See that white oak? Get under the roots. He can't follow us there—his boat's too big."

"Duck your heads!" Sydney headed straight for the huge white oak, forcing the rocking boat in and under the roots and out the other side into another narrow canal.

"Keep going! Keep going! He'll never get through there!"

"But he'll get us on the bay. He knows we have to cross the bay."

They heard a massive thud and a horrible scraping sound followed by the screaming sound of a motor as the intake sucked in air.

"Way to go!" Megan hugged Sydney. "He's stuck."

"Yeah," Luke said. "Or just stalled. But what if he gets out? He's much faster than we are."

"From the sound of his engine, he's well and truly stuck," Megan said. "We'll face it if it happens, and we sort of know the way back, now. We'll go the way he was coming from."

Sydney revved the engine. Sweat poured down her

face. Nothing. The engine roared, spluttered, and died.

"Come on! Come on!" Megan cried. "Let's get out of here!"

"I can't," Sydney wailed. "We're stuck, too." She revved the engine again. Mud flew.

Luke peered through the bushes. "I can see him. He's getting out of his boat."

The clouds that had been rolling in finally opened, and rain poured down. From a distance, low rumbles of thunder echoed, and lightning flickered like blinking neon lights.

Megan pulled Sydney down. "Stay down. Stay quiet. The rain's good. Maybe he can't see us."

"He's coming after us!" Luke whispered.

Together they huddled in the bottom of the boat, partly hidden by the long saw grass and mangrove roots.

Adam groaned and pulled himself up into a sitting position. "Who? Who's coming after us? What's happening?"

"Your Uncle Buddy," Megan said. "Be quiet. We don't want him to know we're here."

Adam's eyes widened. "But he'll help us. Uncle Buddy!" he shouted weakly. "Buddy, we're over here!"

Megan leaped at him and clamped her hand hard over his mouth. "He's a poacher! Adam, he's a frigging poacher! Shut up!"

Through the bushes, she could see Buddy thrashing through the mud. Something flashed in his hand. A gun. Uncle Buddy was armed and after them. So much for family love.

Adam pushed her hand away. "No way. Buddy would never be a poacher. He's going to help us." Weakly, he pulled himself up, waving at his uncle. Megan shoved him backward, and he collapsed back into the boat, groaning and clutching his arm.

Sydney wrapped her arms around Adam. "Sssh."

He stared at her with glassy eyes, and she cuddled him closer, rocking to and fro and stroking his wet hair.

Megan could hear Buddy splashing through the water and saw grass. Had he seen them? "He's coming closer; he's going to see the boat. We've got to get out of here. Help me. We'll try to rock it free. Quick!"

"Look!" Luke pointed. A huge alligator, darker than the shadows, cruised past their boat, weaving its way through the white oak roots and heading toward the thrashing noise up-creek.

"Omigod," Sydney said. "It's heading for Buddy. Do we warn him or what?"

Adam mumbled incoherently, pulling himself up into a sitting position once more.

"Are you nuts?" Luke said. "Let's get outta here. Come on, Sydney. If we get out, the boat will be lighter and then we can push it free."

Following Luke over the side of the boat, Sydney braced herself in the mud. "Ready, set, go!"

Together, Sydney and Luke heaved at the boat, pushing with all of their strength. Rain poured in torrents down on their heads. Each heave pushed Sydney deeper into the mud and deeper into the murky water. Megan watched, petrified. Even if a monster alligator swam right by Sydney or Luke's legs, they'd never see it.

And the alligators could hear them splashing about. There could be another one cruising up right at this moment—a big, hungry alligator, smiling a big, fake alligator smile, just like the one heading for fake-smiling, old Uncle Buddy. She concentrated on watching the water as Sydney pushed the boat again, jumping up and down as she tried to rock it free. "Try it now," Sydney said.

Megan whispered a litany of prayers, one after another, as she revved the motor. With a sucking sound, the boat popped out of the mud, and the engine caught.

"Yes!" Leaping in, Sydney and Luke took a final look at Uncle Buddy.

He was pushing through the mud and saw grass and mangrove roots, heading straight toward them. And, underwater, heading straight toward him, was the dark, torpedo-shaped shadow of the hunting alligator.

"Omigod," Sydney said, taking a quick look back. "That doesn't look good."

Megan shrugged. "It's his problem. Go, go, go!"

Uncle Buddy screamed. Sydney stopped the motor. "It's got him! We can't just leave him."

Adam pulled himself up to his feet, grabbing on to the seat to keep upright. Uncle Buddy had fallen backward into the water and was clinging to the mangrove roots, trying to pull himself up and away. The alligator had its jaws clenched around his upper leg. It started to shake him rhythmically back and forth, back and forth.

The sound of Buddy's screams pierced the air.

"It's going to roll. It'll take him under!" Staggering about as small waves rocked the boat, Adam tipped forward, falling into the water, and flailed his arms as he headed toward his uncle.

Luke grabbed the Red Cross first aid box and flung it as hard as he could. He gave a grunt of success as it landed smack on the alligator's head. For a moment, the thrashing stopped, and Buddy grabbed his chance. He flung his body forward, jamming his fingers into the alligator's right eye.

The beast reared back and opened its jaws, dropping Buddy's leg. As Buddy jumped out of the way, the alligator whipped around and swiped at Adam with its tail, knocking him back in one swoop.

"Adam!" Sydney screamed. "Adam!"

The murky water rippled. For a second, Adam splashed to the surface. Shrieking, Sydney jumped over the side of the boat and splashed toward him. "Adam!" she screamed. "Adam!" Shaking, she pointed into the water. The dark torpedo shape was close. "There it is! It's going after Adam!"

Buddy struggled forward through the water. Bracing himself, he took a deep breath and leaped, landing on the alligator's back. Straddling it, knees gripping the thrashing body, he pressed down on the creature's head and neck, thrusting it down with all of his weight, as his hands inched forward down its jaws. Groaning with effort, he gripped the jaws closed and held tight. Then he clung on, riding the thrashing, wiggling creature, clamping the jaws together with both hands, sweating with strain.

Sydney grabbed Adam, dragging his mostly limp, buoyant body back to the boat. Adam held a shaking arm out toward his uncle, as Sydney pulled him along.

"Just get away from here," Buddy groaned, mud-soaked hair covering his eyes. His blood was soaking his jeans and pooling in the muddy water around him.

"We can't leave without him," Adam gasped.

"Get in the boat!" Luke shouted. "There's more coming."

Massive, scale-armored shapes slid from the bank into the creek and headed toward the swirling bloody water. Buddy's face took on a sick, frightened expression. "Get into the friggin' boat!" he shouted at Adam.

"I'm coming!" Frantic, her fingers shaking, Megan started the motor. As fast as she dared, she made a tight turn in the narrow creek and maneuvered the boat toward Adam and Sydney through the churning water. "Get in!" she screamed.

Leaning down, Luke tugged Sydney into the boat, and the two pulled Adam in, and he crashed headfirst over the side and onto the seat. He lay there, panting.

Megan steered the chugging boat on and over the submerged alligator shapes and pulled up next to Buddy. Buddy slid from the alligator's back into the water, still keeping his hands locked around its jaws. Then, with a heave, he thrust it away from his body as he propelled himself toward the boat and over the side. Standing alert with an oar in hand, Luke shoved the alligator's body and continued striking at anything that looked at all like an alligator. Thrashing about, the alligator made one more swipe, snapping its mighty jaws. Luke thumped its snout. Megan pushed the throttle in reverse. The engine roared.

"Don't stall the thing now!" Sydney screamed.

"You take it!"

Sydney grabbed the wheel. "Do something about that bleeding," she shouted.

While Megan fumbled around for something to wrap around Buddy's bleeding leg, Luke crawled over Adam and Buddy to reach Sydney's side at the wheel and put his arm around her shoulders.

"I think the bay's that way," he pointed.

"Well, I hope Uncle Buddy will be able to show us the way back," Sydney said.

Buddy nodded, shamefaced. "I owe you that one."

CHAPTER 23

"Dad, we're back home, safe and sound," Megan said. "Just chill!"

Thankful to be basking in the sun at the Key West motel's sparkling swimming pool, Megan adjusted her small blue sunglasses and lazily admired the effect of her black bikini, tanned skin, and white ankle cast. They'd be heading back home to California tomorrow. This was the last day of their way-out Florida vacation.

"Chill! I can't believe you'd go off into the swamp like that," her father said. "We were so worried. You're lucky you weren't all killed."

"Yeah!" Megan said. "Poachers! Alligators! Best vacation ever!"

Her mother scoffed, "More like the worst summer ever." Her mother shook her head. "You need to take things more seriously, Megan. You never should've taken that airboat. And you should never have gone off like that without telling us. We've been so worried." She frowned as she looked over at Sydney and Adam, who were sitting side by side at the edge of the pool. Sydney was wearing a "Save the Rainforest" T-shirt over her white bikini, and Adam wore black board shorts, his injured arm wrapped in a sling. "I hope you are taking your antibiotics," she said. "Rattlesnake bites are serious. Adam's lucky that snake gave him only a partial bite."

Sydney shuddered. "Yes, we are," she said. "We were lucky." She leaned against Adam's uninjured arm as they sat close together, their feet entwined under the blue pool water.

"I know I shouldn't have taken the airboat," Megan said. "And I'm sorry. But then I never would have saved Baby Furball from the poachers, so I'm not sorry about that part."

She smiled at Luke, and he grinned back. "Me too," he said. "What'll happen to those poachers?"

"They'll get them, don't worry," his father replied. "Those poachers will be locked up in prison for years and years. I spoke to Adam's Uncle Joe. He used to work for US Fish and Wildlife. He's on his way over here."

Adam nodded. "Uncle Joe is a good guy, but I feel pretty sick about Uncle Buddy."

"It's not your fault," Sydney said.

Adam shook his head. Megan felt sorry for him. His uncle, the park ranger he was so proud of, was an animal poacher.

"Poachers make a lot of money," Megan's mother said. "Sometimes people just can't resist temptation."

"Yeah, but what was up with him? I mean, how far was he going to take it? Would he actually have killed us?"

"I don't know. Maybe he doesn't know either. But he saved you in the end."

"Yeah. After we saved him." Adam winced as he adjusted his sling. "That was pretty intense. I guess he can think about it for a few years in Miami State Prison. I can't believe he'd do all of that. Those poor animals."

"I wonder what happened to smooth-talking Frank after we left him in the muddy hole," Megan said. "You gave him a great whack on his head, Adam. Your aim was perfect."

"Then Sydney whacked the dude again," Adam said, cheering up slightly. "He didn't know what hit him—literally!"

"It was so amazing to see all of you at the top of that hellhole," Megan said. "Oh, look!" She jumped up and onto her good leg. "Here's Baby Furball."

Adam grinned and waved. "And here's Uncle Joe!" he said.

A small, wiry man carrying a little orangutan came walking up to the pool. The dark skin of his face creased into dozens of deep smile lines as he handed the little animal over to Megan, and he went and put his arm around

Adam's shoulders.

"What's happening with Uncle Buddy?" Adam said.

Joe shook his head. "I don't know yet. He's been charged. Buddy will have to pay for his actions. He was a gambler, you know, every night out there at the casino." He walked around the pool, shaking hands. "You guys did a good job. You stopped a nasty poaching ring and saved a lot of animals. Look at this little guy!"

Baby Furball licked the pool water from Megan's arm as she stroked his hair and smoothed out the wild red bangs on his forehead. "Hey, Furball," she said, "I want you to give a cuddle to my twin sister, Sydney the brave and the bold. See? She's wearing a rainforest picture on her shirt just for you. She's the one who saved you from that freaky place. And I'll never call her a wimp or a wuss ever again."

"Gee, thanks." Sydney stroked the little orangutan. "And I won't say another mean word about you. Twin sisters rule."

Megan turned to her father. "Can I keep Baby Furball, Daddy? Please, please, please," she begged.

Her father shook his head. "Not possible, honey. One day Baby Furball will be a great big orangutan."

Baby Furball seemed to know he was the subject of conversation. His little face solemn, he looked from one face to another, then buried his face in Megan's shoulder.

Megan offered him a mango seed and he grabbed it, sucking enthusiastically and then offering it back to her. She took a polite nibble. Her mother grimaced.

"I'd hate for him to live in a zoo," Megan said. "But he's too young to live alone in the wild." She looked unhappily at Baby Furball. "What will happen to him?"

"He needs to roam free in the rainforest," her father said.

Uncle Joe nodded. "Yeah, and we'll do all we can to make that happen. US Fish and Wildlife will do what they can to help the other freed animals, too." He patted Baby Furball's head. "There's an orangutan nursery in Borneo. We'll see if we can get him there. They'll teach this little guy how to live in the wild."

Megan smiled, picturing a nursery full of little red-haired Furballs. "What will they teach him?"

"Lots of things," Joe said. "Where to find his own food and how to build a nest—things like that." He smiled at her. "I still have friends in the US Fish and Wildlife Service. They'll help us find Baby Furball a good place. Maybe you can go over and work there as a volunteer next summer."

"Help at an orangutan nursery! Oh, that'd be wonderful!" Megan hugged the little orangutan tighter. "I'll visit you, Baby. It won't be so bad if I can see you in August."

"I'll visit him," said Luke. "That will be cool."

"Me too," Adam said.

Sydney beamed at him. "Okay!"

Baby Furball grunted and offered Megan his slimy mango seed.

How You Can Help Wild Animals

When the last member of a species dies or is killed, the species is said to be extinct. This means there will never again be another creature of that type on the planet. According to the World Wildlife Fund, 20 percent of all wildlife species could become extinct within the next twenty years.

Let's be caretakers of our world and work to preserve it and all of its creatures. And let's fight to preserve their habitats. Here are some things you can do to save wild animals:

Don't buy items made from the skin or bones of endangered animals.

Don't buy birds that have been captured in the wild.

Don't use chemicals on your lawn or garden.

Recycle papers to save the rainforest, where more than half of all Earth's animals live.

Join a wildlife protection club, like the Sierra Club or the National Audubon Society.

Take part in cleanup days; plastic bags, lines, and plastic rings trap and injure animals.

Provide water in a bird bath.

Build a rock pile for small reptiles to hide in.

Volunteer to help animals.

Become a student volunteer.

Each year, Earth Watch sends out 3,000 volunteers to research endangered animals. For example, in just five years Earth Watch volunteers have saved 33,000 baby sea turtles in St. Croix and turned the beach into a National Wildlife Refuge. You, too, can do things like this!

Adopt an animal. Ask your teacher to help the class adopt an animal:

Adopt an orangutan:
Orangutan Foundation International
www.orangutan.org

Borneo Orangutan Survival Foundation
Orang U Friends Program
www.orangutans.com.au

Adopt a dolphin:
Oceanic Project Dolphin
Oceanic Society Expeditions
Fort Mason Center, Bldg. E
San Francisco, CA 94123.
www.oceanicsociety.org/adopt/adopt-a-dolphin

Adopt a wolf:
https://nywolf.org/support-us/support-us-adopt-a-wolf
https://www.endangeredwolfcenter.org/adopt/

Adopt a whale:
www.adopt-us.whales.org

Ellie Crowe is the author of the following books:

Surfer of the Century: The Life of Duke Kahanamoku

Nelson Mandela: The Boy Called Troublemaker Wind Runner

Harold and the Poopy Little Puppy

Exploring Lost Hawaii: Places of Power, History, Mystery & Magic

Hardcore Inventing: Invent, Protect, Promote, and Profit from Your Inventions

Awards include: Asian/Pacific American Award, Simon Wiesenthal Center/Museum of Tolerance Once Upon a World Children's Book Award, 2010–2011 Texas Bluebonnet Award, Texas Woman's University Librarians' Choice Award, Bank Street College Best Children's Book of the Year, and Hawaii's Kahili Award for Literary Art. https://www.amazon.com/Ellie-Crowe/e/B001JRUWEC http://www.elliecrowe.com

Dear Reader,

If you enjoyed this book, could you please take a minute to write a review on Amazon.com? Good reviews light up an author's life and also tell an author what readers are looking for in a book. And if you have any scary jungle stories or any stories about helping wild animals, please let me know. You can contact me at elliecrowe1@gmail.com. If I use your adventure in the sequel, I'll be sure to credit you. Happy reading!

Ellie Crowe

Connect with Ellie Crowe!
Read All Night Facebook Group:
https://www.facebook.com/groups/517562895306385/

Kid's Book Author Page:
https://elliecroweauthor.blogspot.com/

About the Author

Ellie Crowe is an award-winning author of more than 26 published books. She loves to explore wild places, which led to the creation of her latest book series, *Worst Summer Ever*. The first in the trilogy, *Gatorlands*, was inspired by a trip to the Everglades—while walking along a boardwalk, she was startled to find herself walking over a swamp teeming with alligators! Ellie Crowe lives in Honolulu, Hawaii, and Santa Barbara, California, with her husband and three children.

www.ingramcontent.com/pod-product-compliance
Lightning Source LLC
Chambersburg PA
CBHW070958180726
48291CB00004B/1356